SEA WITCH

This historical romance takes place in an era when transportation was by horse-drawn carriage and when it was not considered right for a young girl to live alone. Thus it was that, upon her grandmother's death, Catherine set forth for Langland Hall to find some cousins who might take her in. Innocent and guileless, it did not occur to her that they might think her a mercenary adventuress and that, instead of finding the peace she sought, she might be throwing down a gauntlet.

SEA WITCH

Iris Gower

This title first published in Great Britain 1998 by
SEVERN HOUSE PUBLISHERS LTD of
9–15 High Street, Sutton, Surrey SM1 1DF.
Originally published 1975 in the USA under the title
Burn Bright Shadow and pseudonym *Susanne Richardson.*
This title first published in the USA 1998 by
SEVERN HOUSE PUBLISHERS INC., of
595 Madison Avenue, New York, NY 10022.

British Library Cataloguing in Publication Data

Gower, Iris

Sea witch
I.   Title
823.9'14 [F]

ISBN 0 7278 2217 9

All situations in this publication are fictitious and
any resemblance to living persons is purely coincidental.

Printed and bound in Great Britain by
MPG Books Ltd, Bodmin, Cornwall.

ONE

Snow hung like lace across the stark branches of the trees, covering the fields with a white silence that was almost alarming, so profound was it.

Inside the coach, I was sheltered from the keen wind, but the cracked and faded leather of the seat carried a chill that seemed to penetrate even to my bones, so that no amount of rubbing of my wrists could produce any warmth.

The horses slipped again, making small, nervous sounds as they encountered the icy patches on the road.

"Good thing when this journey ends, miss."

The only other passenger in the coach smiled at me. He was large and red of face, and I had stared at him so long throughout the journey that I felt I knew him well.

I smiled. "I expect you suffer worse conditions when you are at sea."

He inclined his head in agreement, flattening his greying moustache with the tips of his fingers.

"Oh, yes, indeed I do, but the sea is my element."
He shrugged his broad shoulders. "I never could abide
being shut indoors."

I found myself shivering a little, and even though
the man had been very pleasant company, I found I
had a feeling of mistrust every time I met his eyes.

I glanced covertly at him, trying to discover what it
was that repelled me. Perhaps it was the shifty look
about his eyes, or the way he rubbed his fat hands
together incessantly. In any event, such speculation
was a foolish waste of time; soon I would alight from
the coach and never see him again.

As if in answer to my thoughts, the horses swung off
the treacherous roadway and came to a quivering stop
outside the lamplit entrance of a coaching inn.

"Are we there?" I asked rather stupidly.

The man could not possibly know my destination,
so how could he answer my question? Nevertheless, he
did.

"No, we are not at Swantown yet. Allow me to help
you down. Careful where you place your feet; the
ground is hard with ice."

I stood for a moment shivering in the easterly wind.
"How much further is it, have you any idea?"

He took my arm and hurried me indoors.

"Only about ten more miles. Don't fret; we'll be
there before nightfall."

He settled me before the glowing fire and brushed

the snow from his hat.

"Would you allow me to bring you something, miss? A hot toddy perhaps?"

It really was kind of him to be concerned. I smiled and nodded my head.

"I would be very grateful, thank you."

After all, I told myself, he was old enough to be my father, and I had no reason in heaven or earth to suspect his motives.

He stamped across the room, calling loudly for the landlord. Left alone, I stared into the bright heart of the fire and, unbidden, memories rushed in.

I could again see my grandmother, her eyes sharp and bright like the jet beads that edged her silk apron. I had loved her very much; she was the only family I had ever known. Together we had lived in the mellow rambling house, deep in the quietness of the countryside. It was a peaceful life, and if sometimes I became a little restless, a swift gallop on my favorite grey across the soft rolling fields would quickly dispel any excess of energy.

A coal fell into the hearth, and I suddenly drew back my petticoats, looking around me, suddenly self-conscious about the tears that burned my eyes. Crying would help nothing; my grandmother was gone, laid to rest in the black soil next to her husband.

"Here, miss, drink this; it will set you up a treat."

He towered above me, so close that I could see the red

veins stand out across his cheeks.

"Never let it be said that Daniel Perkins left a lady like you to fend for herself."

"Thank you; it is very kind of you." I sipped the hot drink with enjoyment.

He remained standing before me, and I reached for my reticule with a hand that shook.

"Please, how much do I owe you?" The situation was becoming a little embarrassing.

Perkins flung back his head and laughed. "Independent little thing, aren't you?" He brushed my hand aside. "I'll not take money from you. I still have some sense of chivalry."

He did not take a seat beside me, for which I was grateful. I was in the mood to appreciate a little solitude, so I held out my hand formally.

"I'm Catherine Llewellyn. Thank you so much for looking after me; I really do appreciate it."

He took my hand briefly, seeming somewhat out of countenance. With a last uncertain glance at me, he departed to sit on the other side of the huge fireplace.

It was a relief to sink back in my chair and close my eyes. The journey had been a long one, and I ached to my very bones.

I was almost asleep when I heard the sounds of movement around me. Quickly I rose from my chair, drawing the warmth of my cloak around me.

"We are setting off again, miss." Perkins took my

arm, and I found myself resenting the gesture. "It would not do to be left behind, would it?" He smiled, revealing dark stained teeth, and I hastily averted my eyes.

Outside, I gasped a little as the cold air took my breath away. The sky was overcast, the clouds low as if heavy with rain, and I climbed quickly into the comparative warmth of the coach.

"The last part of the journey now, Miss Llewellyn." Perkins seemed determined to engage me in conversation, and I nodded without replying.

"Don't look so downcast," he said. "You will soon be at home with your folks."

I could think of nothing to say. I pretended to be absorbed in the gathering dusk outside the windows, wondering ruefully what sort of welcome would be waiting for me at Langland Hall.

A feeling almost of panic took possession of me, and I pressed my hands together to stop them from trembling. My cousins would no doubt resent me; why should they welcome me? We had not met for many years, not since I had been a child about five years of age.

Garth and Jonathon Llewellyn—their very names sounded hostile to my ears. I would have remained in Grandmother's house had she not insisted it was not fitting or even safe for a young girl to live alone.

Tears burned my eyes. The old country house would

11

be sold by now. Strangers would walk through the rooms that were beloved and familiar to me, while I would have to become accustomed to a new home reluctantly provided for me by my kinsmen.

It was almost a certainty that my elder cousin would resent me. On his shoulders would fall the responsibility of being guardian to a spinster of eighteen summers.

I did not really look like a spinster. I studied my reflection in the windows of the coach. Dark red curls escaped from under my bonnet, and my face, though ordinary, was not ugly. I had dark eyes like Grandmother, except that mine were over-large for my face, so that I seemed to be an innocent with no more intelligence than a new-born chick.

I closed my eyes, deliberately shutting out thoughts of what the future held in store for me. I was a little warmer now, because of the drink no doubt, and soon tiredness got the better of me and I drifted off to sleep.

I opened my eyes with a sudden pang of fear to hear the driver shout directions outside the now stationary coach. His voice rang out eerily in the sharp night air, and I shivered.

I stumbled outside into the icy coldness of the street and took the heavy bag the driver handed me.

"Anything more, miss?" He was trying to be kind, but I could see he would have his hands full dealing with the restless horses.

"Nothing, thank you," I said with a composure I was far from feeling.

I looked around me eagerly, expecting to see a carriage waiting to take me to my new home, but the road stretched away like a ribbon, deserted and dark.

I moved about a little, unpleasantly aware of the coldness that nipped my face and hands unmercifully.

"You seem somewhat lost, Miss Llewellyn; can I be of any assistance?"

Perkins loomed at my side, looking large and familiar, and I breathed a sigh of relief.

"I was expecting to be met by one of my cousins," I said, despising myself for the catch in my voice. "I am making for Langland Hall; do you know it?"

"Of course." He waved his hand toward a towering mountain that crouched menacingly over the town. "There, right on top of the mountain. You would never make it on foot."

There was a coldness inside me, anger that my own kin could submit me to this ordeal.

I moved my bag to my other hand, uncertain what course to take.

"Perhaps I could find a room in Swantown for the night." I spoke with little conviction, I could hardly expect anyone to put himself out for me at this time of night.

"Left you standing here, have they?" he said abruptly. "The Llewellyns never did concern themselves over much about other people."

"I am sure it has been an oversight on someone's part," I said quickly, trying to hide the dismay his words had caused me. "Probably I am not even expected until tomorrow, I never was very good at organizing."

I stared into the darkness for what seemed a long time, and Perkins remained silent.

"I must walk," I said firmly, although I was trembling at the thought. "There seems nothing else to do."

"I would not advise it, miss." He cleared his throat. "The mists come down very sharply at times, and the paths along the cliffs are unsafe even in daytime."

I was close to tears. I could no longer feel my feet. They seemed frozen solid, and drops of snow fell at intervals from the front of my bonnet.

"You had best come home with me, then," he said at last. "You won't find a palace, but at least you will be warm and dry."

My gratitude was inordinate as I followed him quickly along the icy street, and I berated myself for being uncharitable about his eyes.

He seemed to be leading me toward the harbor, which was no surprise really, because where should a captain of a ship live other than on the seafront?

We passed an ale house, and lights from dozens of candles spilled out onto the street, together with the songs of men somewhat the worse for drink.

I shuddered a little, glad of the company of Perkins. He was forging along at such a pace I could hardly keep up with him.

I don't know how long I walked the narrow twisting streets, smelling of salt with the tang of the sea, but I could actually hear the voice of the waves breaking rhythmically against the shore when we at last stopped and mounted three small steps that led to the home of Daniel Perkins.

Inside it was warm and cheerful, shining with brass and copper and cosily curtained against the cold night air. A young girl about my own age put down her sewing and rose to her feet, surprise written all over her face.

"Where is your mother, Sarah?" Perkins moved toward the fire, holding his hands to the blaze. He did not wait for an answer to his question, which was just as well, as the girl seemed disinclined to make one. "Go fetch her!" he said sharply. "Tell her we have a guest who will need a bed for the night."

I sat rather uncomfortably in the chair he drew forward for me. The girl left the room, but not before I saw a flicker of hostility in her pale eyes.

Mrs. Perkins was a neat woman, almost birdlike in the fastidious way she stepped across the room and took my cloak from me.

"I do not wish to cause you any trouble," I said

quickly. "I would be quite happy to pass the night in this chair before the fire."

Her glance washed over me almost as if she didn't really see me sitting there. Without a word, she moved to the fire and ladled steaming soup into a bowl. She served me first and then saw to her husband.

"The young lady is making for Langland Hall," he said, pleasantly unaware that his wife and daughter both stood watching me as I ate the tasty soup.

"It is kind of you to concern yourself with me," I said, trying to break the rather strained silence. "Perhaps sometime I can repay your hospitality."

The woman stared at me; her round, almost bulbous eyes searched my face.

"I am never likely to go up to the Hall," she said quietly. "The Llewellyns are too grand to entertain the likes of us."

She stared defiantly at her husband. "My Daniel works one of Master Garth's ships. Did you not know?"

"I did not," I said evenly, "though why that should stop you from paying a visit to the Hall I do not see."

She sniffed a little impatiently. "I would have something to say to Garth Llewellyn that he might not like."

"Be silent!" Daniel Perkins spoke quietly, but I felt my nerves tighten at his tone.

When the meal was finished, he rose from the table

and stretched his arms above his head.

"I will go on up to bed," he said to his wife. "See that the young lady is made comfortable for the night." His voice held a warning note, and his wife nodded quickly, anxious to placate him.

She led me through a narrow passageway, holding a flickering candle high, and I shuddered as I glimpsed the quick movement of some small creature along the stone floor.

"You will be all right in the parlor, miss," Mrs. Perkins said quietly. "I'll bring you some warm blankets; you can sleep on the couch there."

I sighed. "I am more than grateful; it is very kind of you to go to so much trouble."

She dipped her thin neck in a bird-like motion and left the room lit only by the one small candle. Wearily I sat down, pressing a hand to my aching brow.

I became aware that someone was watching me, and I looked up quickly to see Sarah staring at me with insolent thoroughness.

I must have looked like nothing on earth; my skirt was crumpled, and strands of untidy hair fell across my cheeks.

"They are not real brothers, you know," she said so suddenly that I was taken unawares.

"What?" I said stupidly. "Whom are you talking about—my cousins?"

She nodded slowly and paused to chew a fingernail.

"The same father but different mothers. Poor Mr. Jonathon is a bastard."

I flinched at her choice of words, but she didn't seem to notice.

"How do you know all this?" My voice was sharp, but though she glared at me for a moment, she answered my question promptly.

"My father told me all about it." Her pale eyes observed me coolly. "They haven't got much money, you know."

There was an assumption in her voice that I would be disappointed by her news, but I smiled inwardly. Not only had Grandmother left me well provided for, but she had made a more than generous bequest to each of my cousins, on one condition only: that the money be administered by me. There was no apparent reason for Grandmother's caution, but she had been a shrewd woman, and I had no doubt that she knew what she was doing.

I had no intention of divulging any of this to Sarah, however. There was a brief silence while she waited to see what I would say, and then, with a toss of her yellow curls, she turned and left me alone.

After a few minutes, during which I sat shivering in the half-darkness, Mrs. Perkins returned with some rough wool blankets which I took gratefully.

Once I lay down on the lumpy couch, my eyes began to close, and in spite of my discomfort, I immediately fell into a deep sleep.

It seemed only a few minutes later when someone knocked on the door, but when I opened my eyes, the grey fingers of dawn were creeping across the room.

"Come along, Miss Llewellyn." Perkins stood framed by the doorway, his face red. "The snow has gone, so your journey should be an easy one."

I made an attempt to tidy myself and went into the welcome warmth of the kitchen, where Mrs. Perkins was busy with breakfast.

"I have borrowed a horse for you," Perkins said. "You can have the animal sent back when you reach the Hall."

I nodded gratefully and followed him outside; obviously there was to be no food for me that morning.

"Here she is." He pulled at the reins, and the animal's head drooped dismally. "Jezebel may be old, but she is sure-footed."

I was still smiling at the incongruous name when Perkins helped me to mount. He handed me my bag and then slapped the horse's rump so that she set off at a slow amble along the cold wet road.

"Goodbye," I said quickly, "and thank you for everything." But my words were in vain. Perkins had already returned to the house and had closed the door on me with a finality that was a little disturbing.

The mare picked her way carefully along the slippery cobbles and then out onto the winding mountain road. At times the track wound dangerously near the sheer edge of the cliff, and as I looked back, I could see the proud curve of the bay hedging the small town I was rapidly leaving behind.

On the water, tall masted ships dipped and rose again on the incoming tide. The view pleased me, and I swung Jezebel around in order to have a better look at it. I pulled hard at the reins and suddenly felt myself slipping sideways. I think I cried out, and then I hit the ground with a bump that knocked the breath out of me, landing perilously near the cliff edge.

Shakily I forced myself to rise and quiet the frightened animal. Someone must have been very careless with the girth to allow it to slacken in such a way. I bent to the mare's steaming flank and saw with horror that the girth had not simply worked loose; it had been deliberately cut.

I looked down at the steep cliff face and shuddered. I might easily have gone over the edge if I hadn't taken it into my head to turn back to look at the view.

The crazy idea popped into my head that someone had attempted to murder me. Then I told myself not to be so hysterical and foolish. Who could possibly want me dead when I did not even know anyone in the town?

I caught the reins in my hand. One thing was certain, I would have to go the rest of the way on foot.

TWO

Langland Hall stood in a hollow of sheer rock that protected the pointing turrets and cast long shadows over the arching windows.

I stood for a moment to regain my breath, trying desperately to tuck my flying hair back under the crown of my bonnet. It was important to make a good impression on my cousins at our first meeting.

"Hello, can I help you? Perhaps you have lost your way."

I turned quickly, startled by the low masculine voice behind me. I was looking into eyes as dark as my own, and somehow I managed to smile in spite of the fact that my breath seemed to have left me.

"I have just come up from Swantown," I managed to say. "Unluckily, I had a fall just down the road a little way."

He examined the mare, who stood docile under his attentions.

"The girth has been cut through," he said, his eyes traveling over me, taking in every detail of my appearance. I nodded.

"That was my own conclusion, but I am not hurt."

He gestured toward the Hall. "Please come inside and take a little refreshment; you must be somewhat shaken."

I realized with a lift of excitement that he must be one of my cousins. I tried to speak, but he was hurrying me toward the ornate doors.

The room which he led me to was large and somber. The furniture, redolent of lavender and beeswax, reminded me poignantly of the home I had shared with Grandmother, and foolish tears stung my eyes.

"You had better sit down. You must have taken a worse tumble than you thought."

Thankfully I took the chair he indicated, wincing a little as my bruised shoulder came into contact with the cold leather.

"You do not choose very suitable weather in which to ride, if you will pardon my bluntness."

He rang the bell and smiled down at me, his eyes holding a challenge that brought the color to my cheeks. He ordered tea, and the fresh-faced maid stared at me with open curiosity as she bobbed a curtsey.

"All right, Lucy; that will be all for now." The twinkle in his eyes belied the sternness of his voice, and, smiling, she left the room.

I looked around me and up at the high ceiling.

"This is a lovely house." I spoke impulsively and so warmly that his eyebrows rose in surprise. To hide my confusion, I crossed the room and looked out across the bay.

"See how the ships stand out so gracefully against the grey of the sky." He stood beside me, and I was acutely aware of his tallness.

"I love ships," I said quickly. "That schooner there is a real beauty."

"You choose well." He smiled slightly. "She is the newest of all my ships, and I have not named her yet. Perhaps I shall give her your name when you can bring yourself to tell me."

My mouth was dry, though I could not think why. I turned to face him, squaring my shoulders.

"I am Catherine Llewellyn; your cousin I believe." It was silly the way my voice shook.

His eyes narrowed, and suddenly I could feel his hostility as he moved away from me.

"This is a surprise. But how did you get here? I can not imagine that you traveled all the way to Swantown on that poor old mare outside."

"Of course not!" I was stung by his tone. "I believed I was to be met yesterday evening. I came by coach, as I said in my letter that I would."

"Letter? But I received no letter. I had no idea that I was going to be honored by your presence."

Lucy came in with the tray of tea, and as if by

common consent we both refrained from speaking, though we continued to regard each other with suspicion.

"Please take your tea," he said as soon as Lucy left the room. Shakily I took up the heavy silver pot and filled both cups.

"Am I to take it there is no welcome at all for me at Langland Hall?" I tried to hide the fear that gripped me behind an air of indifference.

"It is not for me to decide; my brother Jon owns the house." He pointed out toward the bay. "My money is tied up in those ships, so you see I am not a very good catch for anyone."

The innuendo in his voice made my hackles rise. "I agree," I said with all the sarcasm I could muster.

The corners of his mouth twitched a little, and he rocked back on his heels, watching me for a moment.

"Where did you spend last night?" He fired the words at me so suddenly that I was taken unawares.

"Why, at the home of Daniel Perkins." I sounded as flustered as I felt, and he smiled.

"You must have made a good impression on the old sea dog. It is a very rare day when he does somebody a good turn."

"He was very kind to me," I snapped. "If it were not for his help, I should have been forced to walk up to the Hall in the dark."

Before he could say any more, an outer door

banged, and a man younger by several years than Garth hurried into the room. His hair was the same bright color as my own, but whereas my eyes were dark, his were a clear light blue. I identified him even before anyone spoke.

"Ah, you must be Jonathon," I said, responding to the warmth of his smile.

He bowed an acknowledgement and took my hand.

"Why did you not tell me we were to have such charming company, Garth?" he asked, staring reproachfully at his brother.

Garth shrugged his shoulders. "I had no idea, I assure you, though the good lady speaks of a letter. Perhaps you received one?"

Jonathon shook his head. "No, but it is of no importance. We are delighted to have your company at any time."

My heart sank. "But the letter explained that Grandmother was dead and that—" I stopped, not knowing how to continue.

"I think she is trying to say she needs a home." Garth spoke with some amusement, lounging easily against the door frame.

"Then of course she must stay with us." Jonathon spoke without a trace of hesitation, and I could have kissed him for it.

"I have not come empty-handed," I said quickly, wishing to make it clear that I was no charity case, but

Jonathon held up his hand.

"Please, this is your home for as long as you wish to stay; so not another word."

Garth whistled tunelessly through his teeth for a moment and then looked out across the bay.

"Just as long as the place does not crumble around our ears," he said quietly.

Jonathon threw him a strange look and ignored his words. Instead, he took a seat beside me.

"Tell me all about yourself. I do not even know your name."

"Catherine," I said in a low voice. "Catherine Llewellyn. But Grandmother gave me the impression that she kept in touch with you."

Garth looked at us both. "Has Grandmother been in touch with you when I have been out with the ships? Is that where you found the money to keep the house going, Jonathon?"

"No, it is not!" Jonathon turned a white face to his brother. "Do you always have to sneer at everything I try to do? You made no attempt to provide the money I needed, so now you can mind your own damn business!" He turned to me quickly. "I do apologize, Catherine; my brother has no civilized manners. He spends most of his time on his ships, where manners are not needed."

I fluttered my hands nervously. "I did not mean to cause friction between you; perhaps it would be better if I did not stay."

I rose to my feet, not having any idea where I could go, but determined not to stay at the Hall a moment longer.

Jonathon caught my arm. "Take no notice of us; brothers often argue. It does not mean a thing. I will call Lucy, and she will have a room made ready for you." He turned to Garth. "Tell Catherine she must stay with us."

Garth looked down at me with an inscrutable expression on his face. "It would be sheer stupidity to go wandering all over Swantown on your own. Stay with us. We have plenty of rooms which are idle, in all conscience."

It was not exactly a gracious invitation, but then I had the feeling that Garth Llewellyn had little time for the niceties of life. He was a man used to the hardships and hazards of life at sea and had learned to deal only with essentials.

I sank down in my chair, a feeling of despair settling over me, and Garth, with a quick look in my direction, strode out of the room.

"Is it really all right for me to stay, Jonathon?" My mouth was dry as I waited for him to speak.

He knelt before me, taking both my hands in a firm clasp, his eyes regarding me steadily. "I want you here, Catherine, believe me." He chuckled suddenly. "A woman's touch is just what Langland Hall needs.

Can you not see that for yourself?"

I smiled. "You love the Hall very much, and that is something I can see." I gazed around the gracious room with critical eyes. "Everything is in perfect taste, Jonathon, but I think perhaps new curtains would be an improvement." I went to the window and examined the faded drapes more closely. They certainly were shabby. "I could buy some yards of velvet. It would not take me long to make them into curtains, and I really would like to do it."

Jonathon's eyes brightened. "There, you see, you are beginning to like it here. I knew you would."

I laughed and returned to my chair. "That is all very well, but I do not wish to cause friction between you and your brother."

He shrugged his slim shoulders. "We never did get along very well. We are so different. It is sometimes hard for me to believe there is any kinship between us at all."

I watched him covertly for a few moments. He was handsome, much better-looking than Garth. His movements were well defined, as though he would be meticulous in everything he did. And yet there was no pull of attraction for me.

Garth was a different kettle of fish. Immediately there had been a lightning response to his rugged masculinity. His features were autocratic, with almost a streak of cruelty in the set of his mouth and the slant of his dark eyes. I wondered what he would say when he knew that I held a fortune for him, if only he would submit to the indignity of having a woman administer it.

"You need not worry unduly about Garth." I jumped as Jonathon spoke, believing for a moment that I had spoken aloud.

"What?" I asked sharply. "Forgive me; I did not hear you." I smiled to soften the abruptness of my words, and he looked down at me indulgently.

"Still thinking about refurnishing the place," he said warmly. "Well, there will be plenty of time for that later. I was saying that Garth will be away at sea most of the time, so do not concern yourself about his opinions."

To my surprise, I felt a keen sense of disappointment; then I took myself sternly to task. It was none of my business what Garth Llewellyn did, and it was perfectly natural for a sailor to spend his time at sea.

There was a knock on the door, and Lucy came shyly into the room. "I've made up the bed in the front guest room. Master Garth said you liked the sea and would enjoy sleeping facing the beach."

"Thank you, Lucy," I said calmly, though there was a warm feeling inside me at this mark of consideration from my cousin. "Would you mind showing me upstairs now?" I turned to Jonathon. "Is that all right with you?"

He nodded. "Yes, go along. I suppose you want to comb your hair or change your ribbons or some such feminine frippery." He smiled as he saw me to the door. "Make sure you have some rest before you come down again. Do just as you please, and remember this is your home now."

I kissed him quickly on the cheek and hurried up the stairs behind Lucy.

The room was large and cheerful, with bright curtains at the windows and warm coverings on the furniture. The view was breathtaking. The sea dominated everything, stretching away to the horizon, edged with pale sands and rocks that pointed upward like blackened teeth. Over to the left, I could see the harbor with the ships' masts pointing heavenward, almost motionless, as if waiting to be released from an enforced rest.

"Happy?" a voice said near my ear, and I spun round so suddenly that I teetered.

Garth put out a hand to steady me, and I took a deep breath.

"It is a beautiful room," I said quickly. "Thank you for your kindness."

His eyes were unreadable, but the smile that twitched the corners of his mouth was somehow infuriating.

I jerked my arm away from him. "I know you think

I have come here to live off your charity, but it is not true." The words spilled out hotly, but his expression did not change.

"That is just as well, dear Catherine," he said dryly. "Jonathon and I have very little money between us."

I stared at him, my anger dispelled by surprise. "But you do have money!" I was about to tell him of Grandmother's bequest when he strode to the door.

"You might as well believe me now as find out later to your cost," he said sharply. "I have risked all I own on my ships; as for my brother, he has barely enough to keep the Hall from falling into ruin." He stopped at the door. "Take my advice, Catherine. Go somewhere else to seek your fortune; you will find nothing for you here."

Before I could speak, the door was snapped shut. I sank onto the bed, staring blindly before me. It was quite obvious to me now that Garth thought of me as nothing more than a scheming adventuress.

THREE

With wintry brilliance, the sun shone through the small-paned windows, bathing the room in a comfortable warmth. I pushed back the bedclothes and stepped onto the carpet, my gloom and anger of the previous night dispelled.

There was a knock on the door, and Lucy came in, staggering under the weight of two enormous water jugs. Her round, smiling face was flushed from the rising steam.

"Morning, miss." She set the jugs down, sighing with relief, and straightened, her hands rubbing her back in an absent gesture.

"You had better dress warmly, miss," she cautioned. "Even though the sun is shining, there is plenty of frost on the ground."

I made a hasty toilet and, following Lucy's advice, pulled on a good heavy dress that was enlivened by a colorful, embroidered collar.

"Am I late for breakfast?" My fingers were clumsy as I attempted to pin up my hair, and Lucy stepped behind me.

"Let me do that for you, Miss Catherine. I'm quite good at pinning up curls."

I watched in admiration as Lucy deftly worked on my hair, craning my neck to see my reflection in the mirror.

"That's very good!" I said when she had finished. "I've never looked so neat!"

She giggled a little. "It does look nice, miss, even if I do say so myself."

She stood aside to allow me to pass. "There is no hurry, miss; breakfast is late today." She glanced out of the window. "In any case, you have missed Master Garth; he was away to the docks at first light."

There was a strange sense of disappointment in me as I made my way down the sweeping staircase and into the dining room.

"Good morning, Catherine." Jonathon rose to greet me, his eyes looking very blue in the morning sunlight. "I hope you had a good night's sleep."

I smiled." I was most comfortable, thank you. It is a lovely room you've given me."

It may have been my imagination, but a fleeting shadow passed over his face, darkening his eyes. Then he was smiling once more.

"Help yourself to tea, Catherine; please do not stand on ceremony."

I lifted the heavy silver pot and tried to think of

something to say. It was disconcerting, to say the least, to have breakfast with a man who was little more than a stranger to me.

"I used to ride in the morning at home," I said at last, "especially when the sun was shining so brightly."

Jonathon glanced at me sharply "It would be highly dangerous for you to go riding in this weather," he said. "There is a hard frost on the ground, and one wrong move would take you over the edge of the cliff."

I shivered. "I realize that; I almost went over on my ride last night."

His eyes narrowed "Tell me about it, Catherine."

Surprised by the tension in his voice, I obeyed, playing down the fact that the girth had been deliberately cut.

"I very nearly ended up on the rocks." I tried to smile, though the memory of my fright was fresh in my mind.

Jonathon studied me thoughtfully for a moment, and I wondered what was going through his mind.

"I cannot impress on you too forcefully the fact that riding alone here is dangerous." He spoke sternly. "Do not go out in future unless you are accompanied."

Apparently he did not require an answer. He rose from his chair and made a formal bow. "Excuse me, cousin; I have to go out for a while this morning." He managed a small smile. "Will you be all right on your own?"

I nodded eagerly. "Perhaps I can explore the Hall, with your permission, of course."

He hesitated for a moment and then shrugged. "Why not? Please treat this as you would your own home."

On an impulse, I caught his hand. "Thank you for the welcome you have given me, Jonathon." I smiled warmly. "I can not tell you how much I dreaded the thought of coming here. If it had not been for Grandmother's insistence, I would not have found the courage."

He seemed a little embarrassed by my outburst, and self-consciously I drew away from him.

"I must not keep you," I said quickly. "I realize you must have a great deal to do."

He went out without another word, and I stood at the open door, watching, as he rode away down the cliff road. He looked well on a horse; his shoulders were straight and slim, and he held his head high. Obviously, the unfortunate circumstances of his birth did not worry him.

The Hall was large and imposing, and I realized it would take me some time to explore it thoroughly. I pulled a rueful grimace; time was something I was going to have a great deal of in the days to come.

I went upstairs and wandered along the passages; it

seemed that the main rooms faced the sea. The darker, smaller rooms at the rear of the house were used mainly as storerooms. They were uncarpeted and stacked with an odd assortment of boxes. I tried to open one but found it to be securely sealed. I shrugged; it was none of my business anyway, I had no right to be prying into things that did not concern me.

I reached the end of the passage and found a short flight of wooden stairs curving upward. No doubt the top floor had once been servants' quarters, but I guessed that now Jonathon's meager resources would run only to a minimum of staff. Doubtless somewhere below stairs there was a cook and maybe one or two other maids, but so far I had seen only Lucy.

I ventured up the stairs, but found the door above to be locked, and with resignation I retraced my steps.

There was indeed a cook, rotund and friendly, with a broad, good-natured face. She smiled as I entered the heat of the kitchens and continued to knead a piece of dough with strong fleshy hands.

"Miss Catherine, is it?" she said in a soft lilting voice. "You are the spitting image of old lady Llewellyn."

I smiled. "Oh, you knew my grandmother then?" I warmed to her immediately, and she gestured for me to sit at the table opposite her.

"Love you, yes!" She winked at me. "I'm almost as old as she was. Wouldn't guess it, though, would you?"

I shook my head in awe. "No, I would never have guessed it."

She laughed out loud, revealing blackened teeth, and unaccountably, I shivered.

She rubbed her hands on her snowy apron and delved into a cupboard behind her, producing a jar of biscuits with an air of triumph.

"Have one of these, miss, fresh from the oven." She smiled at me as if I were still a child, and not wishing to disappoint her, I took one.

"You'd best go on upstairs now," she said, nodding her head. "Master Garth wouldn't like it if he found you below stairs talking to me."

Reluctantly, I left the warmth and comfort of the kitchen and returned to the sitting room.

It was beginning to grow dark when I heard the ring of hooves against the cobbled yard. I hurried into the hallway, expecting to see Jonathon, but it was Garth who stood looking down at me, his face unreadable in the flickering candlelight.

"The mist is coming down hard," he said, slipping out of his topcoat. "I'm very glad I didn't decide to sail tonight."

He went into the sitting room and held his hands out to the blaze of the fire.

I looked away from him, knowing that even from across the room his dark good looks had the power to thrill me.

After his first remark, he seemed to ignore my presence, and I sat down in a high-backed chair where I could observe him without being too obvious.

His shoulders were broad, straining at the seams of his coat as he moved, and his legs were muscular and lithe as he strode across the room.

The door banged open, and Jonathon, his cheeks reddened by the easterly wind, hurried into the room, going immediately to the wine decanter on the sideboard.

"This is bad weather for man and beast," he said, filling his glass to the brim. Suddenly he turned on Garth.

"Why did you not wait for me? I called to you several times."

Garth looked at him in surprise. "I did not hear you. But then the wind was blowing a gale, so it's not surprising."

Jonathon filled his glass again. "I believe you chose not to hear," he said slowly, his eyes ice cold.

"Don't be foolish!" Garth replied with asperity. "What could be gained by ignoring you?"

Jonathon turned away from his brother, unable or unwilling to answer.

I tried to change the subject. "I have not told you about Grandmother's will," I began. "She has been very generous to you both."

I might as well not have spoken for all the notice they took of me. Garth threw another block on the fire, and Jonathon was busy refilling his glass once more.

"Come, let us not quarrel," Garth said calmly. "I will no doubt be sailing sometime in the next few days; I'll be out of your way then."

Jonathon shrugged. "It was not my intention to quarrel, but I object to being treated by my own brother as an outcast."

His voice rose angrily, and he grasped the bottle of wine and left the room quickly with it under his arm.

I was undecided how I should react. Anxiously I looked up at Garth, trying to fathom his thoughts.

"Don't look so troubled, Catherine," he said absently. "Even the best of friends must have their quarrels."

I nodded. "I understand that, of course." I searched in my reticule for a kerchief, wondering what else I could say.

"Langland Hall is no place for you, Catherine." He spoke so suddenly that for a moment I was not quite certain I had heard him correctly.

There was no laughter in his dark eyes; he was deadly serious.

"But I have no other home." I spoke without thinking, despising myself immediately for sounding so weak.

He raised his eyebrows. "What, no handsome young man waiting to marry you? I am surprised."

I was becoming irritated. "Is it that you do not welcome me here?" I asked sharply, glaring at him so that he was forced to answer me.

"It does not concern me one jot either way," he said reasonably. "I am away at sea most of the time. Still, I say again that this is no place for you to be."

I stood up angrily. "Do not worry, Garth." My tone was stinging. "I have not come empty-handed."

He did not answer me, and his expression did not change by so much as a flicker of his eyebrows.

"It is no concern of mine if Grandmother chose to give you a dowry." He allowed himself a small smile. "I am not seeking a wife, Catherine dear."

I was exasperated. "You do not understand," I protested. "I have money as a gift from Grandmother to you."

"Give it all to Jonathon," he said casually. "His need is greater than mine."

"I do not understand your attitude one little bit." I felt the hot color in my cheeks. "It is not sensible to refuse what is yours."

He shook his head. "I can make my own way in life without handouts from a woman."

"Oh, very well!" I said, my tone sharp. "Have it your own way."

I swept past him and up the stairs, my heart

pounding so hard I thought he would hear it. I could not remember a time in my life when I had been so angry.

My cheeks still burned as I unpinned my hair and kicked off my shoes, sinking weakly into a chair and trying to control the shaking of my hands.

There was a light tap on the door, and I made no effort to rise, believing it was Lucy bringing a warmer for my bed.

"Come in," I said briefly, hoping she would not be long about her business. I wanted to be alone, to give myself a chance to regain some sort of composure.

Suddenly Garth was standing in the doorway, my reticule swinging from his hand, a strange expression in his dark eyes.

"You left this downstairs; I thought you might need it."

I was at a complete disadvantage, with my hair tumbled around my shoulders and my shoes cast off near the bed where I could not reach them.

"Thank you," I said shortly, "but you need not have bothered."

His eyes gleamed in the firelight, and as he came slowly toward me I could not have moved even to save my life. He put his hand at the back of my head and drew me slowly, deliberately toward him.

To my shame, my mouth was as eager as his. I clung to him like a drowning man clinging to a rope, and the moments stretched out into what seemed like an eternity.

He released me gently, a smile turning up the corners of his mouth. "Such fire behind those innocent eyes." He moved to the door once more.

"Sleep well, my dear cousin."

I was alone. I turned to the mirror, and in the flickering light my eyes were black, with purple shadows like bruises beneath them. My hair was tangled, and my mouth drooped like that of a tired child.

"You fool, Catherine Llewellyn," I said savagely, and in disgust turned from my own reflection, slipping between the sheets, grateful for their coolness against the heat of my body.

At last, when I drifted off into an exhausted sleep, I dreamed of Garth, holding me high in his arms, carrying me off to the deck of an enormous ship. And when I awoke, there were tears on my face, though if they were of joy or sorrow, it was almost impossible to tell.

FOUR

It was with difficulty that I persuaded Jonathon to allow me to take the pony and trap into Swantown on my own.

"My dear Catherine," he said patiently, "if only you will give me a few moments, I will take you there myself."

I put my hand on his arm. "Please, it is a fine day with no sign of rain or frost. I promise I will take the greatest care."

He shrugged at last and waved his hands as if giving up. "Very well, go if you must. You are the most headstrong young lady I have ever met."

I gave him no time to change his mind but set off almost immediately down the cliff road. The air was clear and crisp, smelling faintly of spring, although in reality the winter was still upon us, relenting a little on this beautiful morning.

Across the bay, I could see the ships crowding together close to the harbor wall, like chicks around a mother hen. I wondered if Garth was on board his new schooner and if he could be making preparations for another voyage.

My heart dipped at the thought, even though I had scarcely exchanged a word with him after that foolish interlude in my room.

I was determined to put it all out of my mind. He no doubt thought it great sport to dally with me, seeing how inexperienced I was in the ways of men. I pressed my lips firmly together. He would find me foolish no longer.

The curving streets of the town came into view as I rounded the headland. Small cottages leaned drunkenly against each other, and on the corner the bulging windows of a tavern gleamed like eyes in the morning sunshine.

I coaxed the small pony into a faster pace. I had business to do with one Mr. Sainsbury, a banker to whom Grandmother had trusted the handling of her estate just before she died.

"He is a good man," she had said, nodding her head wisely. "And he will be near at hand when you are living at Langland Hall."

Tears came to my eyes. Poor grandmother, little had she known of the hostility Garth would harbor against me and how he would turn his nose up disdainfully at her gift.

I found the office quite easily. It was well situated on a rise in the main street, flanked on one side by a tailor's shop and on the other by an old wine store.

Mr. Sainsbury's brass plate gleamed in the sunlight, and the glass on the door was free of dust, giving me the impression that he was a fastidious man.

And so he proved to be when he ushered me indoors and settled me on the worn leather seat facing his desk.

"Delighted to meet you, Miss Llewellyn. Your grandmother, rest her soul, communicated with me quite often in the weeks before her death." He seated himself where he could have an excellent view of my face, watching my expressions closely as he talked. "She handled her own affairs until she came to me. She was a remarkable woman."

He pressed the tips of his fingers together. "And what can I do for you, my dear?"

I toyed with the lace of my kerchief, uncertain how to begin.

"Come along; I will not eat you." Mr. Sainsbury laughed with delight at his own joke. "Do you need money to replenish your wardrobe? If that is the case, you have only to speak up."

"It's not that," I said slowly. "I was wondering if I could hand over Grandmother's gifts to my cousins immediately."

A frown appeared on his face. "That is out of the question." His tone was severe, reproving. "The understanding is that you administer the money as you see fit."

I sighed. "Well, that's that, I suppose, though it's true I could use a little money." I smiled. "I'm sure you will approve if I tell you I need to buy drapes for the Hall."

He allowed himself a thin smile now that my difficult request was apparently forgotten.

"Yes, I do approve, and please feel free to come to me if at any time you need assistance and advice."

I knew by his tone that the interview was at an end, and a few minutes later, I was outside in the sunshine, my purse considerably heavier. My spirits lifted; it would be fun to choose lengths of material to sew into curtains.

I patted the pony, reassuring myself that he was safely tethered to the stout branch of a tree, and walked happily along the road, glancing into the windows of various shops with childish enthusiasm.

I was beginning to feel hungry and a little tired by the time I had completed my purchases. Slowly I retraced my steps along the street, carrying a large parcel of velvet under my arm.

Suddenly I realized the pony was no longer tethered to the tree where I had left him. I stared in bewilderment around the narrow cobbled street; there did not seem to be any place for the pony and trap to be hidden.

Heavy clouds were rolling across the sky, the best of

the day was gone, and it was growing a little chilly. I shivered, knowing there was only one solution to my problem: I must walk.

Soon I had left the town behind me and was out on the mountain road, struggling a little under the weight of the velvet. I wished now I had not been so eager to bring it home today.

I paused for a moment to recover my breath, moving the parcel from one arm to the other. It occurred to me that Jonathon would probably be very angry with me for losing the animal, but there was nothing I could do about it now.

As I climbed higher, the air became colder, and I noticed that the clouds were gone and the sun was setting in a bright ball of orange.

Suddenly I became aware of the steady beat of a horse's hooves on the hard road. I scrambled quickly up on the small bank at the side of the cliff, leaning back warily against the cool rock. I had no wish to be run over in the gloom.

As a horse and rider appeared over the brow of the hill, I took one look at the broadness of the man's shoulders and knew that it was Garth.

He reined his mount, staring at me in astonishment. "What on earth do you think you are up to?" There was a note of censure in his voice that made my hackles rise.

"Making for home; what does it look like?" I said

with more than a little sarcasm.

With a sigh, he reached down and caught me firmly around my waist, swinging me with ease into the saddle before him. His cheek was against my hair, and with a thrill I felt his arms hold me close to him.

He set the horse into a gallop, and the wind was sharp on my face, tugging at my hair so that it flew in all directions. I turned sideways, and before I knew what was happening, Garth had bent toward me and his lips were on mine, holding me almost against my will.

I tried to pull away from him, but he caught my chin in his hand, and again his mouth was on mine.

When he released me, I could see, far below us, the pointed teeth of the rocks. One false move and we would hurtle to our deaths.

A feeling of wildness filled me; I no longer wanted to draw away from Garth. Brazenly I wound my arms around his neck, clinging to him with all my strength.

For a moment we remained locked together. I heard the wind and the steady clip clop of the horse's hooves, but above all, I could hear the wild beating of my heart. It came to me in a sudden moment of crystal clarity that I was in love with my cousin Garth.

"We are almost home," he said gently, "though I would much rather we were heading for some remote spot where we could be alone."

I stared up at him and saw his eyes flicker toward

mine, and there was something cold about his expression.

"I must make it quite clear I am not offering marriage, my dear Catherine," he said. "I find you attractive, but not so much that I would give up my freedom for you or for any woman."

In silence we completed the ride, and when we were outside the door of the Hall, he lifted me gently to the ground.

"Go inside and warm yourself with a little brandy," he said briskly, "and forget those moments on the road; pretend they had never been."

I flung him a look of bitterness. But his mouth turned up at the corners and, without a backward glance, he urged his horse forward in the direction of the stables.

Clenching my hands together to prevent myself from bursting into tears, I made my way indoors, shivering a little as I closed the large doors behind me.

Jonathon did not take the disappearance of the pony and trap very seriously.

"Do not let it worry you," he said cheerfully. "Anyone in town would recognize the animal and set him on the right track for home."

After supper, Garth and Jonathon retired to the study, and I settled down to try to read a book. Soon I could hear raised voices, and my heart beat unevenly as I realized the brothers were quarreling.

49

I strained my ears, hoping to catch a word or two, wondering if I was the reason for their anger. The door opened so suddenly that I jumped nervously, and Garth strode into the room, his eyes seeming blacker than ever.

"Were you and Jonathon arguing about me?" I said, half afraid to speak lest he bite my head off. He looked down at me in surprise.

"Oh, no, Catherine," he said bitingly. "It was something far more important."

Color flooded into my cheeks. "Do you enjoy being cruel?" I said shakily, and he shook his head.

"Cruel? No, I do not enjoy being cruel, but sometimes you ask for it, Catherine."

"What do you mean?" I demanded, anger rising within me at his tone.

"I mean that you have only been here a few days, and already you are disrupting the household."

I drew away from him, startled by his reply. "I do not know what you mean." I said, "but I do not have to put up with your ill temper."

I ran past him and up the stairs, slamming the door of my room shut behind me.

There was a knock almost immediately, and I made no answer, knowing it was Garth.

He came into the room, and I was furious with myself for not sending him away.

He stood towering over me, and my knees trembled.

"Catherine, I have come to apologize."

He moved toward me, and I quickly stepped around to the other side of the bed. His eyes were dark as they studied me, and then he smiled.

"But I am not apologizing for kissing you, I think you were as happy as I with the situation. Perhaps we should repeat the experiment."

"Please go!" I said sharply. He hesitated for a moment and then shrugged.

"Very well, Cousin, as you wish."

The door closed behind him, and I sank down weakly on the bed, thinking how drastically my life had changed from the peaceful days I had spent with Grandmother.

FIVE

I awoke the next morning to find the whole house in a state of upheaval. Lucy, it appeared, had no time to dress my hair, I must manage my own.

"What is all the excitement about?" I asked, catching her just as she was about to rush from the room.

She lifted her hands in the air. "Mr. Garth is going off to sea on the afternoon tide, and he has given us no warning!" She pushed back a stray piece of hair beneath her mob cap. "I do not know if I am coming or going this morning."

She swept out of the room, and I sat on the bed, staring in consternation at the closed door. How could he leave so suddenly, without even the slightest hint of his intentions?

I must see him. Hurriedly I dressed and, after a fashion, pinned up my hair, caring nothing for the fact that it was already falling from the ribbon.

I met Jonathon on the stairs, and he bade me "good morning" as he hurried past me, dressed in his riding garments.

"The pony is back," he said just before he swung out of the door. "I knew the little beast would return."

Disconsolately I wondered into the sitting room. To my surprise, Garth himself was standing before the fire, a newspaper in his hand.

"So you are leaving today?" I said flatly, not meeting his eyes. "You might have told me yourself."

He raised his eyebrows in surprise. "Surely you will not miss me, Catherine?"

I looked down at my hands, flustered and unable to explain even to myself why I was hurt by his sudden decision to leave.

"I just think it odd that you did not see fit to mention it to me, that is all."

I knew I sounded vinegary, and I half expected the amused smile that touched Garth's mouth briefly.

He came to where I was standing and took my hands in his. I kept my eyes lowered so that he would not know how much I was affected by his closeness.

"Well," I said carefully, "have a pleasant journey." I tried to draw away from him, but he held my hands fast.

"That is no way to make your farewells," he said. "I may never return. I could be lost at sea, anything."

He drew me closer, and I held my breath. But he merely kissed me lightly on my forehead and then released me.

53

The feeling of disappointment made me almost physically ill, and I spun round and left him, tears burning behind my eyes. I would remain in my room until he left, I decided; he would not have the pleasure of seeing how much his departure affected me.

I paced restlessly to and fro, stopping every now and again to look at the waves rushing in across the harbor. It was frightening to think of Garth battling against the elements, so frightening indeed that I longed to run down the great staircase and beg him to postpone his journey until the weather was less cruel.

Somehow I resisted the temptation and sat before the window, telling myself how foolish I was being in giving my affections where they were so obviously unwanted.

I was still sitting at the window some time later when Jonathon called to me from below. I rose to my feet, clutching my fingers together in an effort to stop them from trembling. I felt I could not face the moment of parting and wondered for an instant if I could pretend I had not heard Jonathon's call. But such an attitude was childish, and I forced myself to assume a calm I did not feel as I resolutely made my way down to the hall.

"Ah, Catherine, just in time." Garth smiled down at me from the saddle of his horse, and I saw with bitterness that he had been on the point of riding away.

"Goodbye, Garth," I said, anger making my voice steady. "Be careful; we wouldn't want you to be drowned."

Garth swung his horse around. "Come along Jonathon. If you mean to ride into town with me, you had better hurry. The tide waits for no man."

I watched from the doorway as the brothers rode off down the cliff road. There was not a shred of resemblance between them. Garth, broad of shoulder, sat high in the saddle, while Jonathon beside him was like a slim young boy.

When they were out of sight. I returned to the warmth of the house and wandered into the library, choosing a book at random and attempting to interest myself in the story of other people's lives. The printed words became nonsense before my eyes, and after a while I gave up any pretense of reading and just sat still, thinking of Garth.

Feeling I could bear the inactivity no longer, I pulled on a warm cloak. Perhaps a brisk walk along the cliff top would rid me of my restlessness.

I met Lucy in the hall, and her face furrowed in concern when she saw it was my intention to go out.

"Oh, miss, you'll catch your death on those cliff roads; I'm sure it would be unwise of you to walk in this wind."

"I'll be all right, Lucy." I tried to sound reassuring, but she wasn't convinced.

I smiled warmly at her. "I promise I will be back long before Jonathon returns, and he will never know that I have been wandering around alone."

She shook her head, but I ignored the gesture and went out, closing the door firmly behind me.

I walked along the stony roadway, feeling the bite of the easterly wind, and came suddenly to the top of the headland. It jutted out to sea like a long curved arm, and from it I had a clear view of the ships in the bay, dipping and rising like live birds waiting to be released from captivity.

Somewhere down at the harbor, Garth would be making preparations to sail. The thought was like a stone inside me, and suddenly, almost without realizing what I was doing, I began to run. My feet slipped on the frosty grass, and my cloak billowed behind me, holding me back.

I had no notion what I would say to Garth. In fact, I was not thinking at all; merely obeying some instinct too deep for me to fathom.

It was a foolish and useless venture. Before I was halfway down the road into town, I saw the ships move gracefully out of the harbor before the driving wind.

I leaned against the cliff face, my breath ragged and my eyes burning. The fleet of ships seemed to be poised for a moment, and then they were gone over the horizon, and I had never felt more alone.

I do not remember making the journey home, but I

know that Lucy met me in the doorway, clucking her tongue at my disheveled appearance and bringing me a cup of hot, fragrant tea.

I must have slept a little then, because when I opened my eyes I was aware of Jonathon bending over his desk, writing figures in a long book.

He glanced up and smiled when he saw that I was awake. "Hello, Catherine. Lucy told me you were not well. I hope you feel better now."

I nodded my head, trying to clear the cobwebs from my mind.

We sat in companionable silence, with no sound except for the scratch of Jonathon's pen against the paper and the sound of a cinder falling into the hearth.

I wondered if this was a good time to tell Jonathon of Grandmother's gift. I knew I would have to broach the subject carefully. I did not want him to reject the gift the way Garth had done.

I went and stood near him, and he lifted his head inquiringly.

"Jonathon," I said slowly, "there is something I should have told you as soon as I arrived." I paused for a moment, trying to read his expression, but his blue eyes held interest, nothing more.

"It was Grandmother's wish that we share her estate between the three of us, since we were all the family she had left."

He nodded, still not speaking, and with difficulty I continued.

"There is a drawback, however. I have to administer the money. But you have only to tell me which way you want it spent, and I will see to it."

He smiled. "I will not pretend I do not need the money, Catherine." He gestured around the room. "The Hall eats up the money, and yet I have no wish to see it pass into other hands."

I looked at him in surprise. "Is there any danger of the Hall being sold, then?"

He hesitated for a moment. "No, not in the immediate future anyway." He brushed back his bright hair. "Yet it is true that I do owe a great deal of money for various repairs that simply had to be carried out."

I put my hand on his shoulder. "Well then, Grandmother's money will be put to good use. I'm sure she would have been happy to see it spent on such a worth-while cause."

He frowned for a moment, and then his brow cleared. "I will be grateful to you for your help, Catherine." He caught my hand and, to my embarrassment, kissed the tips of my fingers. Gently I disengaged myself.

"Don't be silly, Jonathon. The money is yours by right; that is the way Grandmother intended it to be. So please don't feel you owe me anything." I smiled at him warmly. "In any event, you welcomed me into your home. I'll never forget your kindness to me when I arrived."

I moved away from him, rubbing my eyes wearily. "I think I'll go to bed; I feel very tired tonight."

He held the door open for me, and I paused for a moment. "Do not sit over those books for the rest of the night; you will ruin your eyesight."

There was an unmistakable twinkle in his eyes, but solemnly he agreed that he would have to stop work soon.

"In any event, you have lifted a load of worry from my mind, Catherine." He smiled down at me. "I will sleep easier tonight, knowing that I can meet my commitments."

On the landing I saw Lucy, who was holding her candle high to light the way more clearly for me.

"I have made a good fire in your room for you, miss," she said, smiling cheerfully. "And there is a warmer in your bed. You will need one tonight; it's very cold in the bedrooms."

"Thank you, Lucy." I said gratefully. "That was very thoughtful of you."

In spite of the turmoil in my mind as I thought of Garth out in the bitter cold on the high seas, I quickly drifted off to sleep, soothed by the warmth of the bed and the friendly crackle of the fire.

It must have been some hours later when I awoke again, uncertain what had disturbed me. I sat up and saw that the fire had burned down to a few embers. Even as I watched, a cinder shifted, falling against the bars of the grate with a faint rattle.

I lay back against the pillows and stared wide-eyed at the darkened ceiling, wondering if Garth would be on watch in the icy coldness of the night.

I heard a voice then, a man's voice, rough with anger. I slipped out of bed, my heart beating fast. With trembling hands I opened the door and silently made my way to the top of the stairs.

In the dim candlelight gleam from the hall, I could see Jonathon, his face white as he looked up at the burly man standing next to him. The man spoke again so suddenly that I jumped.

"You may find that you are in better circumstances now, but don't think you are getting out of your share of our bargain."

I recognized the voice immediately; it was that of Daniel Perkins. I had sat with him too long in the confines of the coach to be mistaken. There was something threatening about the way he leaned toward Jonathon, and I held my breath, thinking for a moment that the two men would come to blows.

"I need the money, I tell you." Perkins spoke again. "And what is more, I need your cooperation. So don't try to wriggle out of anything, or you are likely to find yourself having a nasty accident."

Jonathon's reply was too low for me to hear, but I

could tell by his attitude that he was frightened.

The men moved to the door. Perkins turned for a moment, and his eyes seemed to penetrate the gloom. I drew back in fear, wondering if he had seen me.

The door opened and closed, and shortly afterward I heard the ring of a horse's hooves on the cobbles outside. I wondered for a moment if I should go down to Jonathon and offer my help. But I heard him go into the sitting room, there was the clink of a glass, and I knew he was pouring himself a drink.

Silently I returned to my room, trying to work out in my mind what Perkins could be up to. It sounded as if he were threatening Jonathon with violence. But why? That was something I could not possibly know unless Jonathon chose to tell me.

I crept back between the sheets, but it was a long time before I could forget the anger and downright viciousness that had been in Perkins' voice, and somehow the thought of it brought a feeling of horror that would not be dispelled until the light of dawn spread fingers of light into my room.

SIX

The days seemed to drag, and though Jonathon spent a great deal of his time with me, I felt edgy and strangely lonely, unwilling to admit even to myself that I missed Garth.

The weather had taken a turn for the worse. Driving winds howled around the east wing of the Hall, and sleet tapped icy fingers against the windows.

Prevented thus from walking or riding, I was forced to sit indoors, containing the restlessness within me with great difficulty.

"Is there anything wrong, Catherine?" Jonathon asked at last, and I realized that my constant pacing must be getting on his nerves.

"I hate to be shut indoors," I said apologetically. "If the weather improves tomorrow, perhaps we could ride into town and sort out a few things with the banker."

Jonathon gave me a quick look. "We will see," he said, "but I would not pin any hopes on it. These gales usually last a long time, sometimes for a whole week."

Disconsolately I walked across to the window yet again and stared out to sea. Had I been born a man, I would have been like Garth, free as the air, sailing away whenever the mood struck me. I sighed. I was a woman, and my role was to stay at home at the hearth, content with gentler pastimes.

The morning brought with it a surprise. I awoke to a loud knocking on my door, and before I could gather my wits, Garth was standing at my bedside, a huge smile on his dark face.

He caught a lock of my tangled hair between his fingers, and I stared up at him stupidly.

"It shines like copper and feels like silk," he said softly. Then he seated himself at my side, leaning back in the chair as if he intended to stay.

Lucy came smilingly into the room, a tray balancing on her arm. "Your tea, miss." She glanced at Garth impishly from under her lashes. "You did say it would be all right for me to serve it here, didn't you, sir?"

He grinned. "Yes, I did. And don't worry; I was not going to let my cousin blame you."

I sat up, brushing my hair away from my eyes. "I thought you were still at sea," I said foolishly. "I did not expect to see you for several months."

"Well then, I am sorry if you are disappointed," he replied. "Perhaps you will forgive me when I tell you I've brought you a present from Bristol." He finished his tea and rose to his feet.

"Do not take too long dressing," he warned, "or I might change my mind and not give you the gift after all."

Lucy giggled as she pinned up my hair. "Mr. Garth loves to play tricks on others," she said. "Don't be surprised if he brought you a brace of pheasants or some stone off the beach."

She patted a curl into place. "You have to take him with a great pinch of salt."

I returned her smile. "Thank you for the warning, Lucy. It is just as well to be prepared." I glanced at my reflection in the mirror. "There, I think I will do."

"You look very pretty this morning, miss, if I might be allowed to say so." Lucy chuckled. "Mr. Garth thinks so, too; I can tell by his eyes."

I did not pursue the conversation any further. I was sure Lucy was being romantic, pairing me off with my cousin, but I knew that he had no intention of becoming attached to me or anyone else that I knew of.

In the sitting room, my cousins were standing together before the bright fire, and I could not help contrasting Garth's swarthy good looks with Jonathon's fairness.

"Ah, Catherine, come and enjoy the warmth of the fire."

Jonathon took my arm with a proprietary air that was a little irritating, and I saw Garth's eyes flicker over me with a strange expression in them.

"You should have a fine gown from this," he said, holding out a bolt of shimmering silk. It was a soft muted blue, deepening almost to purple where it fell in folds to the floor, and with an exclamation I caught it between my fingers.

Garth moved suddenly, flinging the silk over my shoulder, where it fell as if molded to my breasts.

"It's lovely!" I said, and in that moment I saw desire for me naked in Garth's eyes. I think I made a slight move toward him, and then Jonathon spoke.

"Very pretty," he said in a surly tone, and I looked at him sharply, wondering if he was referring to the silk or to my foolishness. In any event, the spell was broken, and I wrapped away the silk.

Jonathon put his hand over mine. "Catherine, you do not need plundered silks to make you beautiful." he said, and I glanced fearfully at Garth. His lips were pressed together, and I knew he was very angry.

"Since when have you become the guardian of law and order, brother?" His voice was like a whiplash, and suddenly the room seemed to be charged with emotions that seethed beneath the surface, threatening to break out into violence at any moment.

"I cannot wear it until I have someone make it into a dress for me," I said quickly. "Perhaps Lucy knows of someone in the town."

Jonathon smiled a little, and the tension eased. He

turned away from Garth and spoke directly to me.

"We did promise ourselves a little trip into town. Perhaps we could make it sometime this afternoon, if the weather improves."

Garth frowned and walked over to the window, staring moodily over the bay. I felt somehow as if I'd taken Jonathon's side against him.

"I'll put the silk away safely in my room," I said hesitantly. But Garth paid no attention, and after a few minutes I hurried up to my room, placing the silk on my bed, where it lay like a pool of bright water under the summer skies. Lovingly I touched the smoothness of it, wondering what on earth Jonathon had meant when he had said that the silk had been plundered.

The oppressive atmosphere of the house was giving me a headache, and the sun shining warmly now outside the window seemed to beckon to me. I was quietly leaving the house when I heard footsteps behind me.

"Do you mind if I come with you?" Garth spoke so sternly that I would not have dared refuse him even if I had wanted to. I nodded my head in assent, and with a grim look in his eyes, he held the door open for me.

We walked in silence for a while, the cold fresh air whipping the sparse grass at our feet. I knew that Garth had something he wished to say to me, and my heart beat fast with apprehension.

66

"I trust you realize that Jonathon is very vulnerable," he said at last. "He probably believes himself to be in love with you at this moment, but don't expect the feeling to last."

Anger raced through me, bringing the heat to my cheeks. I clenched my fists, longing to strike the superior look from Garth's face.

"You are determined to think ill of me, aren't you?" I challenged. "You realize now that I am not a fortune hunter, so you assume that I wish to be married."

He looked me over coolly for a moment. "I thought it was every young lady's wish. I'm sure you do not want to be a spinster all your life."

I stopped walking and stood before him. "Don't be so arrogant. Please do not fear for yourself or your brother; I have no plans to wed either of you."

He put his arm around my shoulder in a sudden companionable gesture and, to my surprise, changed the subject entirely.

"Look, there over the bay; see how well my new ship looks?"

I followed the direction of his pointing finger, and indeed, the ship stood out from the rest, gleaming with fresh paint, tall and proud against the old wall of the harbor.

"I mean to take you to see her at close quarters one of these days," Garth continued. "I have named her after you, and she has a figurehead in your likeness."

I stared at him uncertainly. Was he making fun of me, or was he speaking the truth? He correctly interpreted my expression.

"She is high-breasted and small of waist, with black eyes and flowing red curls, just like you." He paused for a moment, staring down at me with a gleam of amusement in his eyes.

"Do you know what I have called her?" He smiled, his teeth very white against the brown of his face. "Sea Witch." He regarded me steadily, and I struggled between laughter and anger.

"If I am a witch, you are a devil. How did you come by the bolt of silk you gave me?"

He stared at a seagull wheeling overhead and was silent for so long I began to think he had no intention of answering me.

"It is as Jonathon told you." He spoke so suddenly that I was startled. "I wait in sheltered coves until a rich merchant vessel founders against the rocks, and then I relieve her of her cargo."

I stared at him, aghast. "You mean you are a pirate?" I drew a little away from him, expecting a denial. It did not come.

"I suppose I am, but then the sailors from the ships think the cargo a good exchange for their lives. They would drown if it weren't for me."

"It is no wonder you do not want Grandmother's money," I said scathingly. "It is too honest for you."

I turned and blundered away from him, not seeing

the heather-covered ground beneath my feet. Long withered stalks of grass caught at my skirt, and occasionally my feet sank into marshy ground. But I ignored the cold wetness and pressed on to higher ground.

The heat of my anger made me oblivious to the fact that the sun had disappeared and the skies had become leaden and ominous. All I could think of was that Garth was a self-confessed plunderer.

It began to rain. Driving, spiteful darts of rain almost crystallized into hail, and above me, mists swirled over the head of the mountain. To my left, I saw a small hollow in the rocks that promised some shelter and, slipping on the wet grass, I hurried toward it.

Huddled there against the cold rock, I had time to look about me. It was obvious that my anger had spurred me on to ground that was quite unfamiliar to me. The empty, desolate hills hunched over me, blotting out the thin light so that I could hardly see my hand in front of my face.

I stood still for a time, waiting hopefully for the rain to ease, but at last I could bear the desolate silence no longer. I pulled my damp cloak around me and headed down in the direction where I thought the road might be.

I heard a call, thin and far away, and with a burst of excitement, I placed my hands around my mouth and shouted back. The voice came again, and then I could hear the faint but distinct beat of hooves.

I hurried toward the sound, stumbling in my relief. A horse and rider appeared suddenly from out of the mist, bearing down on me. I stood there waiting, straining my eyes to see who my rescuer was.

The man was large and high on the saddle, a cloak flowing behind him like wings. He did not check his pace but urged his animal onwards. With a shock I realized that the flying hooves were almost upon me. I threw myself sideways, hitting the ground with such force that the breath was knocked out of me. Struggling to my feet, I tried to run, but the animal had spun round and was heading toward me once more.

"Stop!" I screamed, but my voice was carried away in the mist. In my haste, I stumbled and lost my balance. Then the thundering hooves were so near, it was like the beating of my heart.

I waited until I could hear the animal's breath and then, at the last minute, flung myself away, out of danger for the moment at least.

Slowly I crept behind a boulder, shivering with fear, almost afraid to breathe. I could hear the man cursing as he searched for me. But now the mist was my friend, concealing my hiding place so effectively that at last my pursuer gave up the chase. I lay still for a long time, trying to regain my courage, and then I moved slowly along the ground, following the fresh tracks of the horse down from the mountains.

To my amazement, the tracks led back to the Hall. I went into the welcoming warmth to be met by Lucy.

"Oh, miss, we've all been that worried about you, what with the mist and all." She took my cloak with a disapproving click of her tongue. "You go into the sitting room, and I'll bring you a hot toddy."

I smiled my thanks; the thought of a hot drink was a very pleasant one. I walked quickly into the room, drawn by the large, cheerful fire.

"So you have returned to Langland Hall." The deep voice spoke suddenly at my elbow, and I turned nervously to find Daniel Perkins staring down at me. He moved toward me, a menacing look in his eyes, and I stepped back a pace or two.

"What do you mean?" I asked in a small voice, and he grinned at me in a way that made my flesh creep.

"There is no need for pretense," he said, his glittering, snake-like eyes never leaving me for a second. "You know that I was up in the mountains, too, don't you?" His hand snaked out suddenly and caught mine.

I gave a little scream, and suddenly the door opened and Jonathon, a look of surprise on his face, came across to where I was standing.

"What's going on, Perkins?" he asked in a quiet voice. My arm was released, and thankfully I moved nearer to my cousin.

He put his arm around my shoulder. "Mr. Perkins was just about to leave," he said, and gestured toward the door.

When we were alone, I sank into a chair, and Jonathon took my hand in his.

"There is no need to be afraid, Catherine," he said. "I will always be here to look after you. If only you would agree to become my wife, I could really look after you; you would be safe then."

I sighed. "It's no good, Jonathon. I am very fond of you, of course, but I'm afraid I do not feel love for you." I rose to my feet. "Now I really must go and change my wet shoes!"

I saw Lucy in the hallway. "Would you bring the toddy to my room, please?" I said, and she nodded, following me up the stairs.

The rain was beating steadily against my windows, and I moved over to the fire, taking the drink from Lucy thankfully. She lifted the bolt of blue silk from my bed and placed it on the chest of drawers.

"Isn't it beautiful, miss?" Lucy fondled the soft cloth. "It will look lovely on you. Mr. Garth always did have good taste."

I relaxed in my chair, feeling rather flattered that Garth had given my gift so much thought.

"Do you know anyone who could sew it for me, Lucy?" I asked, rubbing my bruised legs to ease the ache in them. She saw the gesture and, with an exclamation, bent down to inspect the marks.

"My word, miss, whatever happened to you?" Her eyes were large, and I couldn't help but smile in spite of the shiver that passed through me when I thought of those moments on the mountain with the large horse, like an avenging devil, bearing down upon me.

"I slipped; the mist was so thick I didn't know where I was going."

She insisted on bathing my legs there and then, and I did feel pleasantly comfortable after her ministrations.

"Good thing Mr. Garth did not know you were lost in the mountains, miss," she said. "He would have been in a proper state."

"I doubt that!" I said drily. "Where is he now?"

She shrugged her shoulders. "I think he might be gone to the docks; there was some talk of missing cargo. Mr. Perkins came up to tell Mr. Garth about it."

I pondered a little on that. Perkins meant me mischief; that much was obvious. But was Garth involved with him?

"By the way, miss—" Lucy picked up the tray—"I do know someone who will sew your dress. I've just thought of it."

"Oh, good!" I said. "I really must try to rest now; I've developed quite a headache."

She was immediately solicitous. "Try to sleep, miss; you'll be all right in the morning."

My room suddenly seemed menacing to me—a prison from which there was no escape; a place of evil where someone was even now plotting my death.

SEVEN

I drew the pony to a halt outside the address Lucy had given me. The narrow gateway seemed strangely familiar to me, the small house being situated on the seafront near the soft wash of the waves.

My heart turned over with a feeling of horror as I recognized the home of Daniel Perkins. I stood for a moment in an agony of indecision, my heart beating suffocatingly fast.

"What do you want here?" I looked up to see Sarah leaning insolently against the door, watching me. She stepped forward and fondled the pony's ears. "So you've come to see me again," she said softly. "We made Miss High and Mighty walk home last time, didn't we?"

Her eyes were malicious. "You can come in if you like," she said. "My father is not at home, so you'll be quite safe."

"I would like you to explain that remark!" I stepped forward, longing to box her ears, and even though she towered above me, she stepped away a little, alarmed at my anger.

"There's no need to get your dander up!" she said, keeping her distance. "I didn't ask you to come, did I?"

"No, you didn't," I said impatiently. "And this isn't a social visit, believe me!"

She shrugged her rounded shoulders and closed her mouth sulkily.

"I believe your mother is sewing a dress for me," I said cheerfully, pretending not to notice her ill temper. "Could you tell her I have come for a fitting?"

Reluctantly the girl went into the house, leaving me standing outside. I carefully secured the pony to the gatepost.

Mrs. Perkins hurriedly came to the door, jerking her head toward me in a nervous birdlike fashion that still took me by surprise.

"Come inside, miss. I do not know what the girl is thinking about, leaving you to stand outside."

I went through into the musty parlor where I had spent my first night in Swantown, and saw the silk miraculously shaped into a dress.

"I followed the measurements that Lucy gave me, miss, but I will have to fit it on you just to make sure that everything is as you want it."

It took only a few minutes for me to slip off my dress and hold the silk around me, while Mrs. Perkins took in a tuck here and there, deftly placing the pins where they were needed.

She stood back to admire her handiwork and smiled thinly, clasping her bony hands together.

"Very nice it looks, miss; the color is so becoming to your hair. Shows it off a treat."

From some other room I heard a long peal of laughter, and from the way her neck stiffened I knew that Mrs. Perkins had heard it, too. She went to the door and called her daughter.

"Sarah, come here this minute." She glanced apologetically at me and stood tapping her foot impatiently on the floor.

The girl certainly did not hurry. At last she appeared in the doorway and stared insolently at me as I stood carefully holding the blue silk around me.

Mrs. Perkins caught her arm and shook her. "I will not warn you again. I'll tell your father, that I will!"

Sarah pulled away indifferently and tucked a strand of blonde hair back under her cap.

"I was doing no harm," she said lazily. "I was only talking to Mr. Llewellyn. No wrong in that, is there?"

She caught my eye with a look of triumph, and the thought flew into my mind that perhaps she was Garth's woman while he was in Swantown port.

I felt almost physically ill and quickly drew off the silk gown and dressed myself with shaking fingers, acutely conscious of Sarah standing watching me.

"Go into the kitchen and see to your father's

dinner. And stop gawping at Miss Llewellyn. Don't you know it's rude?"

Sarah's lips turned into a smile, and she spun around, leaving us abruptly. A few moments later I heard her giggling once more. How I longed to scratch her eyes out!

"Thank you," I said, trying desperately to see into the kitchen. But instead of taking me the back way, Mrs. Perkins opened the front door.

As I led the pony out onto the street, I tried to turn my thoughts to other matters. I would go to see Mr. Sainsbury and ask him for some of Jonathon's money so that he could start the repairs on the Hall. I felt sure it was a project that would gain Mr. Sainsbury's approval.

As I came level with the office, I could see that it was empty. Mr. Sainsbury no doubt had important business elsewhere, and in a way I was rather relieved. I really was in no mood to concentrate on money matters just then.

I turned toward home, allowing the pony to make his own pace. In my mind's eye was a picture of Garth, his handsome head bent toward Sarah Perkins' blonde one, holding her close in an embrace. Heat rushed into my cheeks as I angrily pushed my thoughts away.

Well, he would see how cool I could be toward him, I told myself firmly. I was no simple town girl to be taken in by his swashbuckling ways.

The sun slid from behind a cloud, warming the air, and I pushed back my bonnet, untying my hair so that it fell free on my shoulders.

I would put Garth right out of my mind! He was a thief, and worse than that, he might easily be a murderer, too. I sighed, knowing that the worst part of it all was his fickleness—the fact that he might have a woman in every port, and Sarah Perkins in this one.

"Catherine, wait!" I looked around, startled. Garth quickly caught up with me, astride his splendid black stallion. "We seem destined to meet on this road," he said, smiling down at me, and I glared at him angrily.

"We could have easily gone into town together," I said icily. "It seems we were heading for the same destination."

He looked down at me with eyebrows raised as if he had no idea what I was talking about.

"I have been at the docks," he said genially. "If it is not a rude question, where were you? I certainly did not see you on the quayside."

I glanced up at him, almost hating him as I again heard Sarah Perkins' silly laugh.

"Someone has been helping himself to my cargo." He was almost shouting above the brisk wind that had sprung up with startling suddenness. "And I do not like it; not at all."

There was a frown between his brows, but I was not

going to be drawn off the tack.

"Looking at the house of Daniel Perkins, were you?" I spoke with all the sarcasm I could muster, and a strange expression came into his eyes.

"I had not thought of that, I must confess," he said slowly, and I shook my head in despair. Lies fell so easily from his lips.

I tried to spur the pony on, but the road was steep, and in any case there was no possibility of leaving Garth's stronger horse behind. He could ride twice as quickly as I if he wanted to.

I did not speak another word to him, even though several times he made some pleasant remark or other. I was determined to put a barrier between us so that he would grow tired of trifling with my affection and leave me alone.

At last the Hall was in sight. I sighed with relief and brushed away his hand when he would have helped me alight from the trap.

"So you are going to play childish games, Catherine." He stared at me for a long moment, and I turned away quickly from the light in his eyes.

"I do not think it is childish to repulse the advances of a thief and a liar," I said with as much dignity as I could muster.

He flung back his head and laughed aloud. "Oh, Catherine, so you are beginning to believe all those stories about me, are you?"

I swept past him into the sitting room, and Jonathon rose from his chair with a welcoming smile.

"I have just this minute come in before you." He poured me a glass of wine. "I took a brisk walk across the hills. It did me a power of good. I feel most refreshed."

Garth eyed him curiously. "I could have sworn I saw you in town." He shrugged his shoulders. "No doubt I was mistaken."

"No doubt," Jonathon said in a tone that implied Garth was prone to be mistaken.

"My dress is almost ready." I spoke quickly, anxious to avert another row. "It will be lovely when it is finished."

My light prattle served its purpose, and Jonathon returned to his chair.

"I am sure you will be beautiful," he said, smiling, "even in that silk."

Garth gave a secret smile, as if he knew something Jonathon did not, and I would have given anything to know what was going on in his mind at that moment.

He gave me a quick glance and, without another word, left the room. In spite of my resolution to be cold toward him, I could not help feeling a disappointment that cast a gloom over the evening when he did not reappear. . . . .

The birds were singing outside my window, and a pale early-morning sun struggled into the room. I became aware that someone was shaking my shoulder, and I turned over, burrowing my head beneath the bedclothes in an effort to cling to the delicious sleepiness that enveloped me.

"Catherine, wake up; it is a beautiful morning for a ride."

I pushed back my tangled hair in annoyance to see Garth bending over me, a look of merriment in his eyes.

"What on earth are you doing?" I said crossly, struggling into a sitting position. "What time is it?"

He placed his hands on my shoulders and drew me toward him, and before I could resist, his lips were on mine and my senses were swimming.

Roughly, I pushed him away. "If that's all you've come to my room for, you can leave now." My tone was biting, and he raised his eyebrows but immediately moved away from me.

"I wanted you to come for a ride. The horses are ready and waiting in the stable; it is going to be a beautiful day."

My head told me I should refuse him, but the temptation to ride with him across the rolling fields was too much for me, and I nodded my head.

"Give me ten minutes to dress. I won't be any longer than that, I promise."

He smiled warmly, and I marveled at his sudden changes of mood. I would never learn to understand him; perhaps that was part of his attraction.

Lucy must have been waiting outside the landing, because as soon as Garth went out of the door, she was at my side, fussing over my hair.

"I wish I had the chance to go out on such a morning with a handsome man like Mr. Garth," she said enviously, and I could not help but agree with her inwardly, although I was determined not to show how pleased I was.

"My grandmother used to say, 'Handsome is as handsome does.' " I could see the glint of amusement in her eyes and I knew I did not fool Lucy one little bit. She could tell how I felt by the way my hands shook as I drew on my soft green riding habit.

I was ready in less than ten minutes, and Lucy stood back admiringly.

"You and Mr. Garth will make a striking couple, and no mistake."

I met Jonathon on the stairs and was embarrassed by his thorough appraisal of me.

"Going riding with Garth, I take it?" His tone was a little cold, and I nodded quickly.

"It is such a beautiful day, I could not resist the idea. Why don't you come along, too?"

To my relief, he shook his head. "No, I have other matters to attend to. Go along and enjoy yourself."

I hurried outside into the chill of the early morning air, and even before I reached the stables, I could hear the ring of horses' hooves on the cobbles.

My heart lifted in excitement, and I smiled warmly at Garth as he came forward to take my hand.

"You look magnificent, Catherine," he said. "Come and see the chestnut mare; I bought her especially for you."

I looked up at him sharply to see if he was making a joke, but there was no sign of a smile on his face.

"Garth, you don't mean to tell me you have bought an animal just for me?"

He waved his hand impatiently and led me to the docile mare standing patiently at the door of the stables.

With Garth's help, I swung up into the saddle and patted the rich silk coat of the animal. She moved a little, and I felt excitement sharpen within me. I longed to give her her head and ride like the wind until both the animal and I were exhausted.

Garth brought his black stallion alongside me, and in the early morning light, he looked every inch the pirate he was reputed to be.

He led the way at a brisk trot, and happily I followed him. The sun was warming as it rose higher in the sky, and the air was sweet like wine, with the faint tang of the sea to give it added spice.

We rode across the fields, and Garth kept to the lowlands, so that we were constantly sheltered from the chill of the winds by the sweeping mountains.

I sighed, feeling happier than I had been since Grandmother's death. Deep in my heart, I knew the reason was that I was at Garth's side.

Eventually we came out of the fields and onto the road winding down to the harbor. I could see the tall ships, stranded by the ebbing tide. The new schooner gleamed brighter than the rest, its masts pointing proudly into the sun.

Garth turned and smiled at me. "I haven't forgotten my promise to give you a closer look at your namesake." He urged his horse forward, and with some trepidation, I followed him.

When we reached the quay, Garth helped me from the saddle, his hands lingering longer than necessary at my waist. I twisted away from him so that he could not see the color flooding into my face.

He took my arm, leading me forward, and all around us was the unmistakable scent of the docks.

Tarred ropes grew hot in the rising sun, and the timber stacked along the wharf lent the air a spiciness that I found exhilarating.

Garth put his arm around me, pointing upward to where the figurehead of the Sea Witch looked down as if in disdain at the activity on the docks. There was no mistaking the red curls and the dark eyes; the figure was clearly in my likeness.

The heat came into my cheeks as I perceived the pink thrusting breasts of the figurehead pointing into the wind.

"Garth, how could you!" I stared at him in horror. "What will the townspeople think of me?"

I put my hands to my cheeks, and Garth flung back his head and laughed.

"It is a very good likeness, as far as I can tell," he said in amusement. "And I don't give a fig what anyone thinks. Why should you?"

"I do care!" I said fiercely. "I won't be considered just another of your mistresses!"

"Worried that your stock will go down in the marriage stakes?" he said sharply, and I glared at him, longing to strike him.

Instead, I turned my back on him and hurried to where we had left the horses. This was positively the last time I would trust him. He would not make a fool of me again.

I spurred the animal forward and rode as quickly as I could along the road back to the Hall. It was obvious that my cousin had no decent regard for me; otherwise how could he make me look like a fool and a wanton in the eyes of anybody who cared to look at his dratted ship?

I flung back my head, telling myself that I cared not a jot what Garth might think of women in general and me in particular. But there were tears in my eyes and my heart was like a stone as I left the quayside far below me.

EIGHT

I did not see Garth at breakfast the next morning, nor did he put in an appearance during the rest of the day. By afternoon, I was miserably convinced that he must have put out to sea again.

Pulling on my cloak, I slipped out quietly, hoping that Jonathon would not notice my absence. I did not feel like a lecture on the dangers of walking alone on the cliffs.

I stepped out briskly along the headland, facing the teeth of the easterly wind that had no right to be blowing on an early spring day.

I stopped when the harbor was in sight, and to my relief saw that the ships were still anchored like a huddle of old women, bobbing on the full tide.

I began to smile, picturing again the figurehead flouting convention, poised above the wharf for everyone to see. Only a man like Garth could get away with such a thing. I no longer felt angry about the figurehead; on the contrary, I was strangely touched that my likeness should take pride of place on Garth's newest ship. If only he had used a little more discretion, I would have been happier.

Suddenly I was laughing uncontrollably. I flung myself down on the coarse grass, feeling the wind tearing at my hair and whipping my skirts into a billowing frenzy. I did not care. I felt alive and light of spirit, and I did not have to look far for the reason. Garth's ship was still in port.

Suddenly I became aware of the sound of horses' hooves drumming along the hill track. I was thrown into a panic of embarrassment, wondering whether to make an attempt to tidy myself up a little or to stay where I was and hope I would not be observed.

There was no more time for thought. I crouched behind a rock, feeling more like a fugitive than a respectable young lady.

Rising and falling on the wind, I heard a man's voice and recognized the rough tones of Daniel Perkins.

"No, the likes of him do not marry! Not with girls such as my Sarah. I will kill the high and mighty Mr. Llewellyn if it is true that he has got my girl into any sort of trouble."

I could not hear the other man's reply. I ventured to raise my head and saw Mr. Sainsbury, the banker, open his mouth to speak, but the wind changed direction and the words were carried away.

They rode on past without noticing me, and I

huddled against the rocks, drawing my skirts around me, feeling suddenly chilled.

Perkins had talked of marriage and trouble, and I thought I knew what he meant. I closed my eyes in anguish, torturing myself with the thought of Garth's lips pressed against Sarah Perkins' full, sulky mouth. I had witnessed for myself how passionately familiar he could be, and no doubt he would promise a simple girl like Sarah the moon and the stars if only she would yield to his blandishments.

I wanted to cry, but the tears would not come. There was a hard knot of pain inside me that nothing would dissolve.

"You are nothing but a fool, Catherine Llewellyn," I told myself, as with an effort I drew myself to my feet and slowly retraced my steps to the Hall.

I had firmly made up my mind to avoid further contact with Garth, but my good intentions were in vain. He failed to return home that night, or indeed for several nights thereafter.

Jonathon seemed more at ease in his brother's absence and freely discussed his ideas for improving Langland Hall. I felt guilty, knowing he was only waiting for me to provide the money so that he could make a start.

I found myself wishing whole-heartedly that I could fall in love with him. He was so uncomplicated and good-humored.

"Catherine, I do not believe you have heard one word I have said."

Jonathon was smiling at me from his high-backed chair near the fire, and with an effort I brought my mind to present events.

"Forgive me; I am a little tired." I made an effort to smile, and he shrugged his shoulders.

"It does not matter. It was nothing of importance. Perhaps you would like a little wine to settle you."

"That would be very nice," I said, more to be sociable than because I really wanted any.

He handed me a glass, and I leaned back in my chair and looked up at him.

"What do you know about Daniel Perkins and his family, Jonathon?" I asked.

He looked at me sharply. "What is there to know? Perkins works for Garth; he has nothing to do with me."

I was a little surprised by the anger in his voice and worried lest he think I was prying into his affairs.

"I just wondered, that's all," I said quickly. "Do you think his daughter Sarah is attractive?"

He smiled and took my hand in his. "Not half as attractive as you are, Catherine."

I looked up at him in all seriousness. "In what way am I more attractive than she?"

He smiled broadly. "You are fishing for compliments, but I will pay them gladly. You are a silk purse and she is a sow's ear—that is the difference."

"You are too flattering to me, Jonathon." I pressed his hand to my cheek, and his fingers were gentle as he smiled down at me.

Suddenly he shuddered, and I looked up at him in surprise, observing his pallor.

"Why Jonathon, what is wrong? Are you ill?" The wine sparkled like liquid rubies as he raised it with shaking hands to his lips.

"It is nothing," he said, collapsing into a chair. "Just a chill. It will pass."

He lay back with his eyes closed, and I saw beads of perspiration stand out on his forehead.

"I will go to bed directly," he said, "and by morning I shall be quite well again." He made an effort to rise, and I pushed him back.

"Stay still while I make sure your room is warm enough. It would do no good to go to a cold bed."

With an anxious backward look at him, I let myself out of the room and hurried, candle held high, up the winding staircase to his room.

The heavy curtains were pulled over the windows, and the light from the fire leaped like frenzied creatures on the walls. I set the candle down and shook up the pillows, finding to my satisfaction that the warmers were in place.

"Well now, what a touching picture!" I spun around to see Garth leaning against the door frame, watching me, his eyes narrowed. "I had no idea you had changed rooms with Jonathon." His smile did not seem at all humorous, and his voice was rough.

"I have not changed rooms. I was merely making sure that all was ready for him to come to bed. He is not well."

He gripped my arm so fiercely that I almost cried out. It was useless trying to struggle, so I remained still, looking at him defiantly.

"Were you intending to warm the bed for him, Catherine? Is that one of your duties?"

I glared at him, anger rendering me almost inarticulate, longing to strike him with all my strength.

"I am not interested in your vulgar opinions," I managed to gasp. "The trouble with you is that you judge everyone by your own low standards. And where have you been for the last few days? Have you no consideration for the feelings of others?" He did not answer, and I spoke again impulsively.

"Perhaps you could help your brother to his room. When I left him, he could barely sit upright in his chair."

Together we managed to get Jonathon to his room. He was trembling as if possessed by the ague, and I did not like the color of his face.

"If he does not improve by morning, I shall ride into town and bring the doctor to him." Garth sounded brisk and not unduly worried.

"Has he been like this before?" I asked, watching him carefully. He did not answer my question, but rang the bell, and after a few minutes Lucy came hurrying into the room.

"Oh dear," she said quickly. "Shall I bring some hot brandy and more warmers for the bed?"

Garth nodded and covered his brother with the blankets. "It is nothing. He will recover in a day or two."

He took my arm and led me outside onto the landing, closing the door carefully behind him. "Let him sleep it off. He needs peace and quiet more than anything."

I was bewildered by the calm way the entire household seemed to be taking Jonathon's indisposition. He had looked almost grey, his hands trembling, and he had been perspiring like a frightened horse.

"Surely you should bring the doctor tonight?" I asked anxiously, but Garth shook his head.

"No," he said deliberately. "Please allow me to know more about my brother than you do, Catherine."

"Why are you so obstinate?" I asked furiously. "Anyone can see that Jonathon is ill!"

"Some people cannot see what is beneath their noses," he said drily, and I stared at him in bewilderment.

He stepped forward and took me in his arms,

92

drawing me close to him, holding me so tightly I could scarcely breathe.

"Your eyes are like jet when you are angry," he said, smiling a little. "And right now there are violet shadows beneath them. Have you suffered a few restless nights since I went away?"

Summoning all my strength, I pushed him away from me, furious at his attitude. "I think I hate you," I said fiercely. "I'm warning you, I do not intend to be trifled with any longer."

He bowed mockingly and turned to go, and the perverse weak creature inside me longed to call out and bring him back.

"You know you do not hate me," he said calmly. "On the contrary, you find me irresistible."

I had no means of knowing whether he spoke in earnest or jest, but anger lent an edge to my voice.

"Barbarian!" I cried, losing my dignity altogether. "You will drive me too far one day."

Lucy appeared on the landing, a bewildered expression on her face, and, shamed to the very core of my being, I covered my face with my hands.

"There, there, Miss Catherine," she said softly, "Come to your room, and I will make you a cup of strong tea. And don't you worry about Master Jonathon; he will be recovered by morning, you'll see."

The tea was hot and refreshing, and soon I managed to smile at Lucy.

"Thank you so much," I said warmly. "My silly outburst was inexcusable. I must be more upset than I realized."

"That's all right, miss," she said, her hands busy folding fresh linen away in the tall chest of drawers. "You should not take too much notice of Master Garth. He has a wicked way of teasing folk. He means no harm by it." She glanced at me, and I could tell by the way her eyes shone that she too was under Garth's spell.

When she left me, I tried to settle down to sleep, but it was no use. My mind turned over and over, thinking first of Jonathon's grey, drawn face and then of the hard, rather impatient way his brother had dealt with him. One thing was clear: Jonathon was given to these sudden, bewildering bouts of illness. Why else should the matter be taken so calmly?

Restlessly I turned over on my side, my eyes drawn to the flickering fire. I felt again the pressure of Garth's lips and the strength of his arms around me, and against my will I trembled with remembered delight.

What was it about my cousin that turned my blood to water in this silly way? The best thing to do was to forget him, put him right out of my mind; otherwise there would be no peace for me.

It was easier said than done, and dawn was spreading pink-tinged fingers into the room before I drifted off into a restless sleep.

NINE

It was in a somber mood that I made my way downstairs the next morning. My hands shook, and I was agitated at the thought of seeing Garth face to face.

I need not have worried. He had had an early breakfast and left the Hall before anyone else was stirring. Lucy was most indignant as she handed me a fragrant cup of tea.

"Bread and cheese left on the kitchen table for any stray mouse to nibble at," she said, her voice rising. "Cook was in a proper panic about it, I can tell you." She shook her head as if Garth's behavior were past her comprehension.

Jonathon entered the room just then, and I was agreeably surprised to see he was almost recovered from his illness of the previous night.

"I can see you are feeling much better," I said with a smile. "Come and sit here next to me and have a hot cup of tea."

I toyed absently with a piece of toast. "Did you

know Garth was leaving this morning?" I attempted to speak naturally, but for all that there was a slight tremor in my voice.

Jonathon shook his head. "I am the last one Garth would confide in, Catherine. Has he gone then?"

"It seems like it." A thought suddenly occurred to me. "It could be that he went into town to bring a doctor for you."

Lucy spoke from behind me, dashing my hopes. "No, miss," she said quickly. "Mr. Garth has taken some clothes from his room; I expect he is aboard his ship by now."

We finished our meal in silence, both Jonathon and I immersed in our own thoughts. At last I rose to my feet, unable to keep up the pretense of eating a moment longer.

"Oh, Catherine," Jonathon said, "I shall be going into town later today. Is there anything you would like me to bring you?"

I tried to think clearly. "No, not at the moment, thank you," I said at last. "But if I think of anything before you go, I'll let you know."

Later, I watched from the window as he rode past on the chestnut mare Garth had bought for me. I felt angry and resentful that he had taken the animal without bothering to obtain my consent. I told myself not to be so petty and foolish; it was a small enough favor for me to bestow when Jonathon had taken me into his home.

The sun was bright on the windows, tempting me to take a walk. I slipped on my cloak, glad to leave behind me the strangely empty aura that now seemed to envelop the Hall.

I walked briskly out onto my favorite path along the edge of the cliffs, breathing the fresh, sweet air that came in off the sea. It was impossible not to be cheered by the warmth and sparkle of the day.

As I rounded the headland, my spirits were dashed. The harbor was empty; all the ships, including the Sea Witch, had sailed. I stared at the wide sweep of the bay, unwilling to believe the evidence of my own eyes, and suddenly I was filled with an impotent rage. Garth must have been preparing for this voyage for some time, and yet he had given no hint of his intentions. How could he be so indifferent, just leaving like that with no warning?

I sank down onto the damp grass, sea, sky and earth whirling about my head in a kaleidoscope of colors, a sick feeling making me dizzy. I laid down my head, feeling unutterably weary, and soon I slept.

When I opened my eyes once more, it had grown chilly; the sea was a dull pewter and the skies were overcast. Gathering clouds indicated that there was a storm brewing, and I scrambled to my feet, brushing the grass from my skirt.

Even as I stood there, large drops of rain began to

fall, and the wind started to howl against the cliff face.

I tilted back my head, looking up into the darkening sky, praying that the storm would pass. In my imagination, I could see the Sea Witch dashed to pieces on the rocks, her masts snapped like twigs.

I pulled myself together, telling myself I was becoming hysterical, a trait I had not previously noted in myself, and set out briskly in the direction of the Hall.

Candles were agleam in all the windows, and for the first time I realized it was almost nightfall. I must have been out on the headland for quite a few hours. I hurried indoors, feeling guilty about my long absence. Jonathon would no doubt be anxious about me.

He came toward me as soon as I entered the sitting room, drawing me into his arms. I leaned against him with my eyes closed, wishing it were Garth holding me with such tenderness.

"Catherine, I have been so worried about you. Where have you been? I have been back from town for hours!"

"I'm sorry, Jonathon, I must have lost my way on the cliffs," I said feebly, unable to tell him the truth: that I'd been pining like a love-sick calf over Garth's departure.

"Come and sit before the fire." He placed a log on the blaze and pulled the high-backed chair nearer the fire.

"Thank you, Jonathon. You always seem to be looking after me," I said with a little smile.

"It is easy to be kind to you, Catherine," he said soberly. "I only wish you would give me more opportunity to show how high is my regard for you."

I looked away from him guiltily. "I would like a hot drink," I said more to change the subject than anything else. He immediately called for Lucy.

"Miss Catherine is going to her room," he said. "Take her some tea up there and make sure the fire is glowing."

"Really, Jonathon," I protested, "there is no need for any fuss. I'm all right, really."

He held up his hand for silence. "You must take my advice, Catherine. I insist."

I gave in with a sigh of resignation, deciding it would do me no harm to have an early night.

Later, as I lay tucked cozy and warm in my bed, I wondered why I could not give Jonathon my love, he was so kind and considerate. All my problems would be solved by such a marriage. Jonathon would naturally take control of the money, and I would have none of the irksome responsibility. I closed my eyes. And though I had been asleep most of the afternoon, I found that I was still tired and soon fell asleep.

I sat up suddenly to find that the candle had burned down. Even as I watched, it flickered and was suddenly extinguished. A board creaked, and with mounting horror, I realized that someone was in my room.

I crouched against the pillows, straining every nerve to hear or see anything that would give me a clue to the identity of the intruder.

Something moved near the edge of my bed, and my hand flew to my throat as I tried to scream.

Suddenly there was cold steel at my throat. Instinctively I turned away, swinging up my arm, and felt the sharp blade cut into my flesh.

A harsh voice uttered a curse, and I found my voice and screamed repeatedly. There was the sound of quick steps, the door was flung open, and suddenly I was alone.

"Catherine!" Jonathon's voice came urgently. "What is happening? Are you all right?"

He came into my room, a candle held high, his face white and drawn.

"Oh, Jonathon, someone was in my room," I gasped. "He tried to kill me."

I fell against him, and he held me tenderly, brushing the hair from my face.

"Wait here, Catherine. I will see if I can catch the intruder."

He hurried down the stairs, and to my relief, Lucy appeared on the landing, her cap awry and her eyes enormous.

"Oh, miss, whatever have you done to your arm?

It's bleeding badly."

She led me back into my room and poured water from the large china jug into a basin. "There, pull back your sleeve and let us have a look at the wound."

She worked with deft capable hands and made soothing noises whenever I winced. Jonathon came back up the stairs, shaking his head.

"I can find no one there, and what is more, all the doors are still locked. It is a mystery." He came and stood at my side. "Are you hurt badly?"

It was Lucy who spoke. "It is just a small cut, Mr. Jonathon, and tomorrow I will put some of my herb paste on it to heal it more quickly."

Jonathon poured us all a drink of wine, and I think he more than anyone needed it. He was still pale, and there were dark shadows under his eyes.

"I think we had all better try to get some sleep," I said, though the thought of being alone was enough to make me shudder.

Jonathon must have seen the movement, because he held out his hand and covered mine.

"Lucy will stay with you for the rest of the night, so please do not be afraid."

He picked up the coal scuttle and built up the fire himself, though I could see that Lucy was itching to take over from him. His efforts were less efficient than she liked to see.

"There," Jonathon said with satisfaction. "You

have plenty of warmth and light, and if Lucy makes up her bed on the sofa, everything should be comfortable for you."

I stood on tiptoe and kissed his cheek, and for a moment there was a strange apologetic look in his eyes. Then he smiled and went to the door.

"Sleep well and do not worry. I will see that we have no more intruders tonight."

I lay against my pillows, glad to see Lucy snuggling under her sheets.

"I hope you are comfortable, Lucy," I said drowsily. To my surprise, I realized I was very tired and would shortly be asleep.

In the early sun of the next morning, the events of the night seemed unreal, almost a ridiculous, impossible nightmare. If it had not been for the throbbing of my arm, I would have doubted the whole thing had ever happened.

I made a careful study of my room, seeking for places where a bulky man could hide, but there was only a large old-fashioned wardrobe, and I felt sure Jonathon would have searched that first of all.

I thought of the incident again in detail—the way the man had loomed large beside me as I crouched next to the tall chest of drawers, and then his oath as I had managed to scream. Something clicked into place, and I remembered where I had heard that voice before. It belonged to Daniel Perkins; there was no mistaking it.

I hurried downstairs and saw that Jonathon had almost finished his breakfast. I sat beside him and began to speak excitedly.

"Jonathon, I know who the intruder was!" My voice was triumphant, and he looked up at me sharply.

"How could you know?" he asked softly. "You yourself said it was too dark to see anyone."

"I know," I said impatiently, "but I have an ear for voices. I can recognize someone more quickly by his voice than by appearances."

Jonathon tapped his spoon against his cup and smiled a little, as if he were humoring me, though somehow he seemed to be ill at ease.

"Well, come along; I cannot wait to hear what Miss Cleverness has found out."

I gave him a quick look. I might be imagining things, but for a moment his tone had been almost derisive.

"It was Daniel Perkins," I said quite sharply, resenting the idea that Jonathon found me a bit of a fool.

He stood up so abruptly that he knocked over his cup and, without noticing the stain spreading across the table, moved over to gaze out of the window.

"Nonsense!" he said firmly, though his hand shook a little as it rested against the curtain.

"It was Perkins," I said quickly. "I was in his

company for quite a long time on the journey to Swantown. I know I am not mistaken."

There was silence for a moment, and I wondered if I had convinced Jonathon that I was speaking the truth.

"Come here, Catherine," he said quietly. Surprised, I went and stood next to him. He pointed across the harbor.

"Tell me what you see?" he said, a strange smile playing about his mouth.

"Just the harbor, of course." I spoke a little impatiently, wondering what on earth this had to do with the intruder of the previous night.

"No ships; am I right?" he said, turning to me with a smile.

The question dropped into my mind like ice, and I saw then what he was getting at.

"Perkins is away at sea." I almost whispered the words, and I realized even as I said them that somehow he had come back last night. It had been Perkins in my room; I was certain of it.

"You see you were mistaken." He stared at me intently, and I could see that my answer was important to him.

"Yes, I was mistaken." I do not know why the words left my lips, but they did, and Jonathon smiled with relief.

"Come, let us have a hot cup of tea and forget all about it."

He led me back to the table, and I pressed my lips together to prevent the rush of protestations that longed to be said.

"I have checked the doors and windows." Jonathon smiled at me. "We will have no more mysterious visitors in the night, so please do not be afraid."

I attempted to smile. Nothing could be gained by insisting that I knew the identity of my attacker. It was better to allow the whole unpleasant matter to drop, although I had a strange feeling that it would not be so easy to forget.

TEN

For several days I was in a state of nervous exhaustion, hardly able to sleep. When darkness fell across my room, I could feel again the cold steel of the blade against my throat. However hard I tried, I could not blot the thought out of my mind that the intruder had been Daniel Perkins.

About a week later, Lucy came into the room, a strange expression on her face.

"You have visitors, miss," she said. "Mrs. Perkins is here, and she's brought that daughter of hers."

"Show them in, Lucy," I said after a moment's hesitation. "It is probably something to do with the dress."

Mrs. Perkins seemed more birdlike than ever; her eyes darted everywhere, and there was a thin smile on her lips.

She stood stiffly just inside the door, but Sarah was bolder. She strode confidently into the room and seated herself comfortably near the fire.

I suppressed the feeling of irritation that was rising

in me and looked questioningly at Mrs. Perkins, waiting for her to state her business. She moved uncomfortably, staring down at the carpet, not certain how to begin.

I tried to help her out. "Have you come to see me about the dress? Has something gone wrong?"

She shook her head. "It's not that, miss. The gown is almost ready; just a few more stitches in the hem is all it needs."

"Well then," I said, becoming a little exasperated, "is there another matter I can help you with?"

I sat down, hoping she would do the same, but she remained standing, and her face grew a shade paler.

Sarah was staring about her with avid curiosity. There was something unpleasant in the way she seemed to be summing everything up.

"Please sit down, Mrs. Perkins," I said sharply, and she was so surprised that she sank down on a chair near the door, her mouth hanging open as she stared at me.

"Sarah will have money soon," Mrs. Perkins said, and I frowned, trying to understand what she was talking about. She pointed at her daughter, and for a moment there was a spark of feeling in her pale eyes.

"Oh yes?" I said uncertainly.

"My Sarah will be a fine lady quite soon now." She smiled proudly, and Jonathon's words popped into my mind. He had called Sarah a sow's ear, somewhat unkindly perhaps. But a fine lady she would never be by any stretch of the imagination.

Mrs. Perkins seemed inclined to talk now that she had started, and I let her ramble on, hoping to find out what she wanted of me.

"So you see, miss, it would only be a loan, just for a little while until Sarah's married." She looked at me hopefully.

Then it occurred to me that she was trying to borrow money on the strength of her daughter's expectations, whatever they might be.

I watched Mrs. Perkins rubbing her thin hands together and felt more than a little sorry for her. She couldn't have much of a life with a man like Daniel Perkins to contend with, as well as a spoiled, difficult daughter.

"I'll be glad to help you," I said briskly. "But you will have to wait a little while, say until the day after tomorrow. Will that suit you?"

"You are too kind, Miss Llewellyn," she said so quietly that I hardly heard her. "I will have your dress ready when you call."

As I watched them both walk away from the house, I shook my head in bewilderment. I couldn't actually pin down anything Mrs. Perkins had said. For instance, how much did she need?

I shrugged and closed the door. Tomorrow I would go into town to see Mr. Sainsbury, and until then, I would put the entire Perkins family out of my mind.

I would have liked to discuss the incident with Jonathon, but I saw very little of him that day. He was probably on business. I went up to my room and sat in the window seat, looking out over the sea. Not even to myself would I admit that I was hoping for the sight of sails appearing on the horizon. But the stretch of ocean remained flat and empty, glinting gold under the sun.

I leaned my face against the cool glass and found myself remembering vividly how it felt to be in Garth's arms. It was so lonely at the Hall without him.

I brushed the tears away from my eyes, impatiently telling myself how foolish I was being. It was obvious that I was over-tired; a peaceful night's sleep would do me a world of good.

The next day I was determined to keep myself so busy that no thoughts of Garth would be able to invade my mind. I dressed in my riding habit and, without asking permission, took Garth's stallion out of the stable.

As I rode away from the Hall, I thought I glimpsed Jonathon from an upstairs window, and I wondered guiltily if he had wanted the stallion for himself.

Mr. Sainsbury was pleased to see me. He invited me to sit down and was so pleasant and charming that I wondered what he could have in common with a man like Daniel Perkins. They had seemed to be on close terms the day they had ridden past me on the hill road.

"I would like to have some money," I began, and he nodded solemnly, a slight smile on his face.

"Of course. Why else would an attractive young lady like yourself come to visit a crusty old man well past his prime?"

I laughed, appreciating his good humor. "I think I shall want quite a lot," I said. "There are repairs to be done at the Hall, and putting money into something like that is a very worthwhile cause, don't you think?"

He nodded ponderously and opened the drawer in front of him, putting his signature to a thick document before looking up at me again.

"This entitles you to draw up to two hundred pounds from the money held in trust by me. Is that sufficient?"

I nodded. "Oh yes, I think so."

In my mind I was doing a quick calculation. If I offered Mrs. Perkins a quarter of the money, there would be enough left for Jonathon to pay off some of his creditors.

Soon the business was transacted, and I said goodbye to Mr. Sainsbury, taking a deep breath as I went into the brightness of the mid-morning sun.

The stallion was contentedly chewing the sweet spring grass, and I decided to leave him there and walk the short distance to Mrs. Perkins' house.

She looked at me in surprise, and I wondered with irritation why she was always so vague.

"May I come in?" I asked at last, as she stood staring at me in apparent dismay. She moved aside and allowed me to enter, and I walked before her into the small, cramped parlor.

Sarah came and leaned against the door, watching me with a look of amusement on her face.

She examined every detail of my appearance, her dimpled arms folded over her large breasts so that the material of the gown was pulled tight, emphasizing her curves.

Mrs. Perkins flapped her hands helplessly. "Go and get some work done, Sarah, there's a good girl," she said pleadingly, and with a sniff the girl moved away.

"Now then," Mrs. Perkins said, "what can I do for you?"

I stared at her in astonishment. "I thought you wanted help." My bewilderment must have been obvious, and she flushed a little, avoiding my eyes.

"I don't know what you mean, miss, I'm sure," she mumbled. And I noticed her thin hands were trembling.

I sat down in consternation. "You wanted a loan," I said more bluntly than I'd intended.

She shook her head. "No, not me, miss," she said. "I never asked you for nothing."

"But you said it would only be until your daughter

111

became a lady. I distinctly remember." I was becoming exasperated, and my voice was rising a little.

Mrs. Perkins' eyes inexplicably filled with tears. My anger evaporated, and I shook my head, completely at a loss.

"Do I understand that you no longer want any help from me?" I asked more gently, and she shook her head dumbly. "Very well then." I got to my feet. "We will say no more about it. I must have been mistaken."

Mrs. Perkins seemed unable to pull herself together, and I walked to the window to give her time to compose herself.

My gown lay in a shining, neatly folded bundle, and I picked it up with a gesture of pleasure.

"How lovely it looks!" I smiled, and Mrs. Perkins dipped her head.

"It is almost finished," she said quickly. "Perhaps you had better be going now, Miss Llewellyn."

She looked around uneasily, and I felt a prickling sensation as if someone unseen were watching me.

"I must pay you for your work." I reached for my reticule, but it was not where I had left it. "Where is my bag?" I said anxiously. "There is a great deal of money in it." I moved a plump cushion to look behind it.

"I did not see you bring it in." Mrs. Perkins' hands were fluttering in agitation. "Please, I don't want you to pay me for the dress. It's quite all right."

"Oh, but it isn't as simple as that," I said firmly. "I know I had my reticule when I came in here. We must find it."

Sarah was suddenly in the doorway. "Is this what you are looking for?" she said, her eyes unreadable. "You should take better care of your belongings, but then, them as has plenty don't have to worry over-much, do they?"

I took my bag without a word and pressed some coins into Mrs. Perkins' thin hands.

"Thank you for sewing my gown so beautifully," I said. "I'll stop by and collect it in a week or two." There was no response from her, and with a shrug I turned and let myself out into the street.

It was a relief to be heading for home once more. I simply could not understand Mrs. Perkins' attitude. If she had wanted to borrow money from me, why refuse it now? It just didn't make sense.

I went over and over the conversation we'd had the previous day and realized she hadn't once asked me outright for the money.

I sighed. Perhaps there had truly been a misunderstanding, but in that case, why had Mrs. Perkins and Sarah come up to the Hall to see me?

The questions turned round and round in my head, refusing to be answered, and I put the horse into a fast gallop to clear my head a little.

Jonathon was working at his desk when I arrived home. He stood up at once and smiled at me.

"You've been out enjoying the morning sun, I see." He took my arm and led me to a chair.

I smild as I anticipated his pleasure. "I've brought some money for you. You can get on with the repairs you wanted to do."

He moved away from me. "You are sure the money is mine?" he asked abruptly. "You aren't giving me charity, are you, Catherine?"

I sighed. "What is wrong with everyone today? No one seems to want money!"

He looked at me quickly. "What on earth do you mean?" He bent over me, concern on his face. "Who has been asking you for money?" He frowned, and his eyes were clouded.

"Just a little joke," I responded. I put my arm around his shoulder. "Jonathon, the money is yours. Grandmother meant for you to have it."

On an impulse, I brushed my hand through his bright hair, and he caught my fingers, kissing them gently.

"Won't you marry me, Catherine?" His forthrightness took me unawares, and the color rose in my cheeks.

"I don't want to be married to anyone just yet, Jonathon," I said firmly. Yet I knew that if Garth wanted to marry me, I'd be the happiest girl in the world.

He sighed and grasped my shoulders, his blue eyes suddenly intense. "I'd look after you and be good to you, Catherine. I wouldn't go chasing off to sea like Garth."

I tried to wriggle free, but he still held me. He was stronger than I would have given him credit for.

He drew me toward him, and his lips touched mine briefly, gently. I was filled with compassion, because I knew he would never have the power to stir my blood as his brother did.

I put my hands on his face and looked him straight in the eyes. It would be more honest to tell him how I felt.

"I think very highly of you, Jonathon," I said, "but I could not marry you. It just would not work. Don't you see? I would make you a very poor wife."

"Let me be the judge of that," he said, and there was a sudden coldness in his voice.

I shook my head. "It's no use, Jonathon. I don't love you." He jerked away from me, angry color rising to his face.

"Very well, Catherine!" he said. "Be it on your own head, then."

He left the room, slamming the door shut behind him, and I sank down in the chair, wondering what he had meant by that strange remark. It sounded almost as if, by refusing him, I were going to bring retribution upon myself.

115

But that was an absurd assumption. He was merely upset, which was natural enough in all conscience. I was allowing myself to become fanciful.

I picked up my reticule and drew out the bag of money Mr. Sainsbury had given me. For some reason it did not seem quite so full now. Carefully I began counting and eventually found that there were fifty pounds missing.

I saw again in my mind's eye Sarah insolently holding my reticule in her hand. There had been every opportunity for her to steal some of the money.

I was becoming heartily sick of the whole business, and I wished for the hundredth time that Grandmother had left everything to my cousins.

I sighed and went upstairs to change out of my riding habit. There was nothing to be gained by sitting brooding about what couldn't be changed. I would be better occupied turning out the cupboards in my bedroom.

I slipped out of my clothes and stood for a moment in my shift, looking out over the sea. There was an emptiness inside of me—a longing that was like a pain—and I knew that if I could only see the tall sails of the Sea Witch approaching the harbor, all my melancholy would vanish.

Such thoughts were merely daydreams. Even if Garth did return home tonight, he would still be the same man who had trifled with my feelings and then insulted me. Nothing would change him or make him love me.

I flung myself on the bed, covering my face with my hands. I loved Garth and I wanted to be loved in return. But I might as well wish for the moon for all the good it would do me. Tears burned my eyes, but determinedly I sat up and washed my face in the scented water from the jug on the table. I would be a fool to cry over Garth Llewellyn. I'd do better to remain a spinster.

Some hobgoblin of mirth came alive in me then, and I sat on the edge of the bed, laughing like a child. Somehow, in the days since Grandmother had died, I had lost my sense of fun. I was becoming old before my time, dry as dust, taking life and myself too seriously.

Garth had the right idea. Live only for today, and let tomorrow take care of itself.

I combed my hair and put on my prettiest dress. Even if I could not feel gay and carefree, at least I could try to look it.

I went to the cupboard and began to empty the contents onto the floor. If my hands were busy, perhaps my thoughts would give me some peace.

ELEVEN

Dusty and tired, I surveyed the pristine cupboard with some pride. It had taken me several hours to clean away all the accumulated dust and cobwebs and the stack of papers that had been strewn untidily on the shelves, but the effort had been worth it.

Carefully I stacked the papers into a pile and put them in a drawer. I had no time to go through them at the moment, and I doubted they were of any consequence anyway.

At the very back of the cupboard I found a portrait of a mother and child. Black eyes stared up at me, and the slightly arrogant mold of the mouth was unmistakable. The small boy was Garth, without a doubt.

The woman was something of a surprise. She had a fine high forehead, and a mane of thick black hair cascaded to her shoulders. She looked foreign, Spanish perhaps. It was obvious she was Garth's mother.

Gently I rubbed away the dust and placed the

portrait on a table near my bed. The colors glowed with life, and it seemed strange to me that such a magnificent painting should have been hidden away.

There was a sudden knock on my door and, startled, I spun around to see Jonathon smiling at me.

"Tea is ready, Catherine." He smiled. "You've been working away like a mouse for so long I wondered if you had fallen asleep!"

Laughing a little, I drew him into the room. "Look what I have unearthed, Jonathon," I said proudly, and pointed to the portrait.

He uttered an oath beneath his breath. "I thought that had been disposed of a long time ago," he said sharply. "Come along downstairs, Catherine; you must be thirsty after all your work."

He looked back at the portrait, and I felt he wanted to destroy it.

"What's wrong?" I asked, and he shook his head.

"Nothing you need concern yourself with," he said rather harshly. "Don't look so alarmed; you may keep the painting if you wish."

It was good to sit before the fire, drinking the hot, fragrant tea. I closed my eyes for a moment, and Jonathon leaned forward and took my hand.

"There, I knew you would over-tire yourself," he said reprovingly. "Why did you not tell Lucy to clear out the cupboard for you?"

"I am not tired," I protested. "On the contrary, I

was just thinking of going for a short walk to refresh myself."

I expected him to make an attempt to stop me, or at least suggest that he come with me, but he merely handed me ny cloak and warned me to keep away from the cliff edge.

"Don't go into the mountains," he added. "You can't trust the mists at this time of year."

A sharp wind had risen. It whipped my cloak around my shoulders and tore the ribbons from my hair, and I walked briskly in an effort to warm myself.

The moonlight was silvering the sea, and silver foam lay like a bracelet along the line of the shore. I strained my eyes, hoping for a sight of a ship, but there was nothing but the sea and the sky and the wind.

I retraced my steps after a while, and when I neared the Hall I saw that candles had been placed at the windows. It was a welcome sight, and I realized suddenly that I had grown to love the mellow building in the short time I had lived there.

I let myself into the warmth, brushing back my tangled hair. Of Jonathon there was no sign, and I surmised he must have retired to his room shortly after I'd gone out,

Lucy popped her head around the door. "You're back then, Miss Catherine," she said brightly. "Would you like a toddy to warm you? You look fair frozen?"

"That would be very nice, Lucy." I smiled at her, "It's kind of you to think of it."

She blushed with pleasure. "It was Cook's idea, I must confess," she said. "She's taken a real fancy to you, she has, and that's not usual for her.

"Tell Cook I'm flattered." I stretched my hand out to the warmth of the fire. "And I would be very grateful for a hot drink."

I read for a while, trying to lose myself in the adventures of the fictitious heroine. The trouble was that she could immediately sum up a situation and then act on her intuition. My own intuition seemed to have deserted me.

At last I gave up in despair and went to bed. My last thought before I went to sleep was of Garth. I hoped with everything that was in me that he would soon return from his voyage.

The next day I felt so ill that, when Lucy came to bring me breakfast, I could hardly lift my head from the pillow.

"Why, Miss Catherine!" she said in surprise. "You are as red as a lobster; you need something to cool you down."

She soaked a cloth in the scented water in the bowl on the dressing table and placed it on my head.

"I'll mix you up some medicine that will bring your temperature down," she said briskly. "I'm a great hand with herbs."

I was too weak to argue with her and somehow managed to force down the evil-smelling liquid that she brought me.

Jonathon came to see me, an expression of concern on his face.

"Lucy told me you were not feeling well," he said softly. "I knew you weren't up to walking about in the chill night air, especially as you'd been turning out the cupboard like a servant girl."

He sat down beside me and took my hand in his. "Promise you won't act so foolishly again?"

I nodded. I would have promised anything so that I could be left in peace.

There was a noise in the doorway, and the color drained from my face as I saw Garth leaning against the wall, a strange expression on his face. I knew how the situation must look, with Jonathon at my bedside wearing his robe.

Jonathon was apparently unmoved by his brother's abrupt return. He rose to his feet and welcomed Garth with a great deal of calm and very little enthusiasm.

"So you are home again?" he said. "Have you had good pickings, or were there no sinking ships to plunder?"

He might as well have saved his breath, because Garth ignored him and spoke directly to me.

"It did not take you long to become on intimate terms with my dear brother, did it? Well, I think you deserve each other."

He turned on his heel, and I could hear the sharp tap of his boots as he went away along the corridor.

Jonathon shrugged. "Don't let him upset you," he said. "Garth makes it almost impossible for anyone to like him."

I wanted to protest that I loved Garth and would have done anything to prevent his believing that Jonathon and I were on imtimate terms.

"I'm very tired," I said instead. "If you will excuse me, Jonathon, I will rest for a while."

He nodded immediately. "Of course, Catherine. It was thoughtless of me to stay so long when you are not feeling well."

He took my hand, turning it over, and with a flourish, kissed my fingertips. "Try to sleep now, and don't worry about a thing."

I sighed with relief when the door closed behind him. Jonathon was very sweet, but at the moment I could not cope with his advances.

Later Garth came to my room, seeming to fill it with his rugged masculinity. His dark hair was crisp and shining, and his very skin seemed to radiate good health.

"I'm sorry for my ill conceived remarks," he said at once. "Lucy has told me that you are feeling ill. Shall I send for a doctor?"

I shook my head. "No, it's nothing; just a chill. I'll be up and about again in a few days. Don't worry."

He sat beside me, and my heartbeat quickened. I

looked away again quickly, in case he sensed my thoughts.

He placed his hand on my brow. "You are very hot, Catherine. I think it would be just as well to ask Dr. Millar to call." He moved to the door, and I could see his mind was made up.

When he had gone, I lay back and closed my eyes, and it seemed that I was floating away above the Hall, soaring like a seagull over the creamy breakers.

I was faintly aware of a cup being held to my lips, and then I drifted off again to my own private dream world.

The candles were flickering above me when I opened my eyes again, and a strange man was leaning over me, a bland expression on his face.

He took my wrist in capable fingers and smiled down at me.

"You young ladies do not wear enough clothes to keep out the chill wind," he said reprovingly. "But a few days in bed will do you a world of good, and you'll soon be on your feet again."

He moved away from the bed, and I saw his grey head bent close to Garth's as they discussed me in whispers. The doctor lifted his hand in farewell. "Good day and obey orders, young lady."

I attempted a smile, but already the mists seemed to be returning before my eyes. I closed them, and the mist was still there, so I gave myself up to it.

After a few days, my strength returned, and Garth

insisted on carrying me downstairs and seating me in the sun shining in through the window. I could see the Sea Witch, her paint somewhat dulled but as proud as ever, rising on the swell of the ocean.

"It is a lovely day," I said softly. "I wish I could be out on the headland feeling the spray in my face."

Garth sat beside me. "Too much of that has been your downfall. You just do not realize how treacherous the weather can be at this time of year."

I looked up at him. "But I feel wonderful now. It was just a chill, after all."

"A chill perhaps, but it could have led to pneumonia if you had not been so well looked after."

I was warmed by his concern, and he must have seen how I felt, because he looked down at his brown fingers.

"Anyone would have done as much for you, Catherine." He moved away from me. "Do not allow yourself to read too much into my actions."

My happiness burst like a bubble. He was telling me that he was motivated by duty, nothing more.

"Thank you anyway," I mumbled. "I am indebted to you."

He shook his head. "No such thing. Don't be so foolish, Catherine."

Weak tears sprang to my eyes. He was determined to make light of what he had done so that I would not feel obligated to him in any way.

Jonathon came into the room just then, a smile of

delight on his face as he saw me seated in my chair.

"Catherine, how well you are looking!" He drew up a chair beside me. "How would you like it if we gave a small supper party for just a few guests?" He was like an eager boy, trying hard to please.

"That would be very nice." I tried to infuse a little warmth into my voice, but the thought of meeting people was almost enough to make me feel ill again.

"Don't you think it a bit early to encourage visitors?" Garth asked flatly, and Jonathon stared up at him almost with dislike.

"We will hold the party sometime next week," he said quickly. "All Catherine will have to do is to be her usual charming self."

"I shall enjoy it," I interrupted quickly before the cousins could start quarreling again. "I shall have to wear my new dress if it is ready."

I smiled at Garth. "The silk you gave me should look wonderful; I shall be the belle of the ball!"

He stared moodily over my head. "I still think it is too soon for Catherine to be subjected to the ordeal of facing your friends," he said pointedly to Jonathon. "Are you showing her off as your future wife perhaps?"

My heart twisted at his words, and I stared at him, hoping for a sign that he would object to such a course of action. After a moment's hesitation, Jonathon took my hand.

"I would be only too delighted to make the occasion

a celebration if only you would agree to become my wife."

He looked at me with such depth of feeling that it was hard for me to answer. He took my silence as encouragement and leaned forward to kiss me on my cheek.

"I know I should have waited until we were alone to ask you, Catherine, but I have no objection to Garth being the first to know."

Events seemed to be like a flood tide, lifting me and carrying me off my feet, and I felt too weak to protest.

I looked toward Garth, but he was staring out of the window as if none of it were any of his concern.

"If that's what you really want, Jonathon," I said quietly and allowed him to kiss me gently on the lips. It was a chaste kiss, more that of a brother than a lover, but somehow it moved me almost to tears.

Garth rose abruptly and smiled bleakly at me. "I suppose I may be allowed to congratulate you?" He stepped forward, and then his lips were on mine, and for a moment I clung to him.

He moved away, and there was a strange look in his dark eyes. "Now I know how Judas felt," he said curtly, and went out, slamming the door after him.

Jonathan shook his bright head. "I can never make him out; he talks in riddles."

I knew what he meant, however, and there was a deep pain of unhappiness lodged within me as I allowed Jonathon to take my hand once more in his.

TWELVE

The pony trotted briskly, enjoying the sparkling warmth of the day, and I hadn't the heart to curb him, in spite of the fact that the trap rocked perilously over the uneven road.

It was good to be away from the oppressive atmosphere of the Hall, where Garth spent most of his time avoiding me and Jonathon fussing over my health. It was a miracle that I had been allowed out alone.

As I drew nearer the town, the houses on the seafront looked crisp in the sun, like icing on a cake. The tide, rolling gently into the harbor, was aquamarine under the cloudless sky.

I climbed carefully down from the trap, unwilling to admit even to myself that my legs were still a little weak from my illness, and fed the pony an apple. A group of ladies from the town walked past me, staring at me rather curiously, I thought, and looking away when I smiled at them.

With a shrug, I went into the store. I wanted some

spices and a jar of peppers; that was all Jonathon would allow me to carry.

The chatter of conversation stopped for a moment as I entered and then, as if by a signal, started up again. I asked for the goods I required, and the rotund little shopkeeper hastened to serve me.

"It is not right to give service to those who associate with thieves and murderers!"

I spun around quickly to see a small elderly lady, dressed from head to foot in black, staring at me with burning eyes.

"Are you speaking to me?" I asked in surprise, and she moved closer, staring into my eyes.

"I don't say it's your fault; you look harmless enough. And Mr. Jonathon, he's a good man. But that half-breed brother of his, he's a bad one all right!"

Shaking, I picked up my purchases and went outside, my eyes blinded for a moment by the dazzle of the sun. I stumbled toward the trap and climbed inside. What on earth was the old lady thinking of, calling Garth a thief and a murderer? I sat still for a moment, the reins idle in my hands. Perhaps that was what he was after all. Hadn't he confessed to me that he plundered ships for their cargo? Might he not leave the stranded sailors to their fate?

I shuddered a little; the warmth had gone out of the day for me. Still, there was one errand that had to be done. That was to collect my gown from Mrs. Perkins.

She answered my knock straight away, almost as though she had been waiting for me, her bulbous eyes darting around furtively.

"Come inside," she said, and the moment I stepped over the threshold she slammed the door shut.

"What on earth is wrong?" I asked in exasperation. "Everyone is behaving so strangely."

She looked at me vaguely. "I don't know what you mean, miss," she said, the color sweeping up from her thin neck to her forehead.

"Oh come now, Mrs. Perkins." I said impatiently. "Your husband works for Garth Llewellyn. Surely he knows something about the talk that is going on in the town."

She sniffed nervously. "Mr. Perkins has not been out with the ships for some time now, miss. There is no way that he can be blamed for any goings-on."

She handed me a parcel. "Your gown, Miss Llewellyn. I hope it fits well, because I can do no more work on it." She ushered me to the door, opening it just enough to allow me to pass through and then closing it again in my face.

Shakily I sent the pony off at a trot up the hill. I looked back down the hill, and the clouds rolling in from the sea made the houses look dark and forbidding, very different from when I had approached them earlier.

There was a shout up ahead of me, and the pony

pulled nervously at his reins. Four burly men blocked my way, shirt sleeves rolled above brawny elbows, an evil-looking bunch.

One came alongside me. "So this is what Garth Llewellyn's harlot looks like with her clothes on," he said, his blackened teeth showing in an evil grin.

"I've only seen your likeness on the front of the Sea Witch, and I wondered if the real thing was as pretty."

He burst into laughter, and the other men looked on with interest to see what I would do.

Taking a deep breath, I tried to be calm. "Would you please allow me to pass?"

For a moment, the man was so surprised that he almost moved out of my way. With a snarl, he caught my arm and twisted it.

"Miss High and Mighty, is it? And who are you to order good honest seamen around?"

I tried to pull away from him, but he caught my face in such a grip I thought my jaw would break. He put his arm around my waist and swung me to the ground, pulling my bonnet roughly from my head and flinging it away.

"See what pretty red hair she has!" He caught a lock of it, twisting it cruelly so that my head was forced back and I had to look up into his face.

"You wait!" I said fiercely. "When Garth hears of this, he will have you flogged!"

The man flung back his head and laughed. "Hear

that, lads? She's threatening to tell on us!" He leered down at me. "And what do you expect Llewellyn to do? We have enough on him to send him to prison for many a long year."

"Liar!" I shouted, beating at him with my fists. "He has done nothing wrong."

I was no longer sure about anything, but I was compelled to defend Garth against these thugs.

"Give me a kiss and I'll tell you all about your fine lover," the man said loudly, and I tried to twist away from his thick, revolting lips.

"All right!" he said with venom. "I'll tell you anyway." He smiled unpleasantly. "Garth Llewellyn has brought opium into this country, selling the stuff down the coast of Wales as if it was no more harmful than sugar sticks. He has even made his own brother a victim of his greed."

"It's all lies!" I said. But inside me there was a terrible dread as I remembered Jonathon's strange bout of illness and the casual way Garth had treated it.

The man pressed me to him. "I like spirit in a woman; it adds spice to the dish." He pushed me down into the grass and caught at my bodice with rough hands, tearing the material easily. He laughed as I struggled beneath him; his hands were at my throat.

"We'll show you what we do with loose women in

Swantown," he said harshly. Suddenly I was frightened. I felt his weight upon me and realized that my struggles were in vain. I looked up at the face above me and knew that appeals for mercy would be useless. I lifted my head and screamed with all my might. Then I saw his huge fist beat down upon me, and everything became a whirling blackness . . . .

When I regained consciousness, I saw that I was lying in the trap, and Jonathon was bending over me, covering my torn bodice with his cloak.

"What happened. Where have those men gone?" I asked hysterically, and Jonathon patted my shoulder reassuringly.

"I heard you scream," he said, "and when they saw me coming they turned and ran."

I stared at him in disbelief. The men who had accosted me certainly didn't seem the sort who would run away from one man alone.

He must have sensed my thoughts, for he drew a pistol from his belt. "I think this helped to persuade them!" he said with a smile.

He climbed onto his horse and took the reins in his hand.

"You just rest," he said. "I'll lead the pony for you."

I struggled to sit up and winced a little at the pain in my face. I put a tentative hand to it and felt that it was swollen.

"Have the townspeople all gone mad?" I said, speaking with difficulty, and Jonathon turned to look at me.

"Don't think about it any more," he said gently. "You'll soon be safely home."

As I stared in silence at his slim back, I wondered if it was true that he could be taking opium. I shuddered. Surely Garth would never harm his own brother.

Suddenly I felt ill. I lay back as Jonathon had advised, trying to overcome the waves of faintness that threatened to overwhelm me.

The journey seemed never-ending, but at last the pony and trap came to a halt outside the Hall.

Garth hurried out and exclaimed in horror when he saw my face.

"My God! What has happened to you?" He cradled me in his arms and carried me indoors, and tears came to my eyes at his gentleness.

"Some men from the town set about her," Jonathon said. "It was very fortunate that I heard her screams; otherwise who knows what would have happened?"

"Is this true?" Garth demanded, and I nodded my head without speaking.

"But why should anyone do this to you" He looked at me in bewilderment, and I sensed the seething anger.

"They were angry with you," I said at last. "They

think of me merely as your woman."

He set his lips in a hard line, and his knuckles were clenched so that the skin shone white.

"I'll kill them!" he said between his teeth. "Just tell me who they were, Catherine."

I shook my head. "I don't know, and in any event you cannot fight the whole town. They have all turned against you, it seems."

I stared at him. "They say you are a peddler of drugs. Is there any truth in that?"

His face seemed to pale beneath the tan. "Do you have to ask me that?" he said bitterly. "I am a lot of things, most of them bad, but I do not prey on people who are too weak to protest."

He held my eyes, and it was I who turned away. Just then Lucy bustled into the room with a tray of tea.

"Master Jonathon tells me you had a fall from the trap, miss," she said. Then her eyes became round with amazement. "Oh, my good Lord!" she said.

I got to my feet unsteadily and looked at myself in the mirror over the fireplace. The entire side of my face was one black bruise, and my eye was almost closed.

Lucy came to my side. "I'll bring some witch hazel for you; that should ease it a bit."

I sank back into my chair, holding my cloak self-consciously around my bare shoulder.

"Help me to my room, Jonathon," I said unsteadily, ignoring Garth, who was standing near the window. "I'll have my tea there, Lucy, if you don't mind."

It was a relief to climb into the comfort of my bed. I ached all over, as if a horse had stepped on me.

Lucy held up my torn dress, a strange look in her eyes. Without a word she folded it up.

I closed my eyes, aware that my head was pounding, and pressed my hand over my eyes, trying to stop the ache.

"I'll bring you some herb tea, miss," Lucy said with compassion, and silently left the room.

Lucy's potion really did work. I slept like a baby and awoke the next morning feeling well rested and almost back to normal. I looked in the mirror and saw that, though my face was still bruised, the swelling around my eye had almost gone.

Garth and Jonathon looked at me in surprise when they saw I was dressed and up and about. The aroma of toast made me realize suddenly how hungry I was.

Garth rose to his feet and held out a chair for me. "I'm going down to the docks in a moment or two," he said, and my heart missed a beat with fear for him. "I don't want you to go into town under any circumstances, do you hear me?"

I nodded meekly, and Jonathon put his arm around my shoulders.

"I'll look after Catherine," he said quickly, and there was a sudden shadow on Garth's face.

"Oh, excuse me," he said sarcastically. "I forgot that you two were betrothed."

He stamped out of the room, and Jonathon shrugged his shoulders.

"Garth cannot help his surly manners," he said in a tone that was meant to be comforting. But in the mood I was in, it merely irritated me.

"In any event," Jonathon continued," we will not have to put up with him for very much longer."

"What on earth do you mean?" I asked in sudden fear, putting my hands around my cup as if to draw warmth from it.

Jonathon looked up quickly, his blue eyes narrowed as he searched my face.

"I just mean that he will be returning to sea within the next few days. What on earth did you think I meant? For a moment you looked at me as if you had seen a ghost!"

There were beads of perspiration on his face, and he brushed his hand across his eyes as if he couldn't focus properly.

"Are you all right, Jonathon? You are terribly pale." I moved toward him, but he shook my hand away.

"Of course I'm all right." He stumbled to his feet. "I just need a little air."

Anxiously I stood at the window and watched him stagger out onto the lawn. He looked like a man who had drunk too much wine.

I clasped my hands together, trying to think what I should do. I wondered frantically if Garth was still at the Hall. It did not seem likely, as he had said he was going down to the docks.

Jonathon was out of sight now. He had rounded the shoulder of the building, and I thought with a sudden pang of fear that he might make his way down to the cliff road and, in his unstable frame of mind, stagger over the edge to his death.

I hurried outside. The sky was overcast, and the air carried rain with it.

"Jonathon!" I called, and my voice seemed to be carried away thinly on the wind.

I came upon him suddenly. He was slumped against the wall, a peaceful look on his face as if he were asleep, although his eyes were wide open.

"Are you all right?" I touched his sleeve carefully and waited with bated breath to see what his his reaction to my interference would be.

He said nothing, and I could see that his eyes were uncomprehending.

"Come with me, Jonathon." I slipped my arm around him, almost dragging him to his feet, and with difficulty made my way inside.

Lucy put her hand to her lips when she saw us,

staring a moment before coming to Jonathon's other side and helping me take him to his room.

Neither of us spoke, and I knew that the same dreadful thought was in both our minds. Had Jonathon been taking opium?

I returned to the sitting room and sat in the window seat, my spirits so low I was almost on the verge of tears. My body ached from the rough treatment I had received from my unknown assailants on the road, and my head pounded.

Perhaps it would be better for me to go away from the Hall, start a new life on my own. I had enough money to support myself for some time to come.

Even as the thought came, I rejected it. I could no longer imagine a lifetime spent apart from Garth, even though I knew he was a womanizer and probably worse.

I stood up restlessly. I had promised Garth I would stay indoors, but I longed to be free, to walk out onto the headland in the teeth of the wind and watch the breakers curl, only to dash themselves into a thousand pieces against the jagged rocks.

I forced myself to walk to the bookcase and choose something that would hold my interest. For once I would obey Garth and be sensible.

Determinedly, I seated myself in a comfortable chair and turned the pages. But after only a few moments, the book had fallen into my lap and my thoughts were spinning around in my head like rats in a trap.

Later, in the middle of the afternoon, Jonathon came downstairs, obviously recovered from his illness, a smile on his face as he came to my side.

"Are you feeling better?" I asked nervously, and his eyebrows shot up in amazement.

"I feel fine, on top of the world. Why do you ask?"

I shrugged helplessly. It was clear that he remembered nothing about the events of the morning.

He took my hand in his. "You are so solicitous, Catherine," he said. "When are you going to become my wife?"

I pulled away from him, startled. I knew I had been wrong ever to let him think I could marry him.

"I cannot marry you!" I said vehemently, and something flashed for a moment into his eyes, a look that took me by surprise so that I recoiled.

"I'm sorry," I said more quietly. "I should never have allowed you to think that I would become your wife."

He stared at me coldly, and his hands shook as they rested on the arms of his chair.

"Very well, Catherine, I will not ask you again," he said, and his voice was almost devoid of expression. Suddenly I was afraid.

"I do not mean to hurt you, Jonathon," I said quickly. "It is just that I realize I do not love you the way a wife should love her husband."

He stared over my head. "You love Garth," he said in the same flat voice. "He always manages to take everything I want."

"You have the Hall," I said gently, knowing how much he loved the fine old building. But even in that assumption I was wrong.

"Oh yes," he said. "I have the Hall. It eats up money; it is like a living monster devouring me."

I rose to my feet, making an effort to keep some semblance of composure.

"Jonathon, you have not been well. Perhaps if you rested in your room for a while, you would feel better."

He slumped forward suddenly, his head on his arms in a childish gesture that moved me strangely. But one thing was certain. However much I might pity Jonathon, I would never marry him.

THIRTEEN

To my amazement, Jonathon had decided to go ahead with the arrangements for the dinner party. He politely asked me to go down to the kitchens and inform Cook that she should use her best, most elaborate recipes.

There was an odd look on her broad face as she listened to me, and when I lapsed into silence she merely nodded her head, pursing her lips as she returned to her cooking.

"Is there anything wrong, Cook?" I asked shakily, and she shrugged her round shoulders.

"It isn't for the likes of me to say anything, but Mr. Jonathon is asking for trouble, that's what I say."

There seemed nothing further to add, and I retraced my steps up the wooden staircase.

Jonathon was obviously waiting for my report. "I gave Cook your instructions," I said, avoiding his eyes. "But she didn't seem too happy about it."

"She is not here to be happy," he said shortly. "She must do as she is told."

"Jonathon," I said tentatively, "don't you think it would be better to postpone the party, for a little while at least?"

"Nonsense!" he exclaimed. "Why should I? It is not me the townspeople are angry with."

He sat down at his desk and drew some papers toward him, turning his back on me as though the matter were settled.

I stared out of the window, longing to take a walk along the headland, but the rain was streaming down the windows, and the wind howled around the corners of the building like a stricken animal.

I moved to the fireplace, my nerves on edge, and Jonathon frowned at me.

"Can you not find something with which to occupy yourself?" he said not unkindly. And like a drowning man, I clutched at straws.

"I will go up to my room," I said quickly, and before he had time to make any protest, I hurriedly left him, feeling suddenly released.

Lucy had just built up the fire. She rose to her feet, smiling at me, a streak of dust across her face.

"Oh, miss, you did give me a fright!" she said. "I thought some restless spirit had come to haunt me when I heard the rattle of the doorknob."

I smiled. "I'm a restless spirit all right," I said, "but one very much of this world and glad of a good fire on a day like this."

Lucy winked. "I expect you could drink a cup of tea if I made one, couldn't you?" She moved to the door. "I might even get Cook to give you some of her fruit cake."

"That would certainly be nice, Lucy." I sank onto the bed. "It was kind of you to think of it."

I pulled a chair up to the fire and sat with my feet on the brass fender, listening to the rain dashing with frenzy against the small panes of the windows. It was a good thing that Garth was working at the docks and not out at sea; otherwise I would not have had a moment's peace for worrying about him.

A coal dropped from the grate, and a flutter of paper caught my attention. I leaned forward and saw that it was part of a letter, browned by the heat but still readable. It said:

"To my precious son, Jonathon, I leave the residue of—" The rest of the words were too charred to be legible. I turned the paper over, wondering where it had come from. Suddenly I thought of the box of papers under my bed and scrambled down onto my knees, knowing before I looked what I should find. I was right. The box was empty; my hiding place had not turned out to be a very secure one.

When Lucy returned with my tea, I searched in my mind for a way to interrogate her about the papers and at last came right out with the question.

"Lucy, did you move some papers from under my bed?" I asked, and she turned to me quickly.

"Yes, I did, miss. They were some things that Master Garth wanted me to burn. Was there anything there you wanted, then?"

I shook my head. "No, not really. They didn't

belong to me; I had no right to keep them."

She placed the tray before me, smiling as she held out a plate heaped with fruit cake.

"I told you before that Cook liked you, didn't I, Miss Catherine?" She looked triumphant. "This is some of her special cooking; you're very honored." She laughed wickedly. "Cook can be a regular vixen if she chooses to be, but she is good to them she likes, I'll say that for her."

"Give her my thanks, Lucy," I said. "Won't you stop and share my tea? I'll never get through it all alone."

"Love you, miss, I've got my work to finish!" Lucy said with good-humored reproof in her voice. "I've got to hurry back to the kitchens at once, or I'll be in for it."

It was miserable sitting alone in my room, but anything was preferable to spending my time in Jonathon's company. I leaned back against the curve of the chair and closed my eyes. So suddenly that I jumped guiltily, there was a loud rapping on my door.

"Come in," I said in a voice scarcely above a whisper. To my great relief, it was Garth who opened the door.

"Why are you shut away in your room?" he asked in concern. "Are you not well?"

"I'm quite all right," I said quickly. "Would you like some tea? Lucy just brought me some."

He sat down and stared at me, a little bewildered by

my attitude.

"You are definitely not yourself, Catherine," he said, staring at me with unblinking eyes. "Perhaps you should go away from the Hall for a little while. I'm sure you would benefit from a change of scenery."

Even though he was voicing a thought that had been mine only a short time before, I felt suddenly angry.

"You want me out of the way, is that it?" My tone was sharp, and he looked at me in surprise.

"Catherine, believe it or not, I am only thinking of you." His tone was gentle. "It could be that you are in danger here."

"Oh, that is rubbish and you know it!" I said. "What on earth has given you that idea? Is it just because of that bunch of thugs who waylaid me outside the town?"

He shook his head. "Not just that, Catherine." He brushed his fingers through his hair. "I can't explain. Won't you take my word for it?"

"Why should I take your word for anything?" I was so angry I could have hit him.

He reached out suddenly and drew me to him, and before I could move, his lips were on mine, warm and demanding, drawing every ounce of strength from me.

He released me as suddenly as he had held me, and I could think of nothing to say. He took my hand, his expression difficult to read.

"Catherine, I will have to go away again quite soon, and I am reluctant to leave you alone."

I stared at him foolishly, trying hard to regain my wits.

"But I won't be alone," I said. "Jonathon will be here."

He shrugged. "Yes, Jonathon will be here." He looked out at the driving rain for a moment.

"You must always be on your guard, Catherine," he said. "Will you promise me not to do anything foolish?"

As I nodded, he moved toward the door, a frown still between his eyebrows.

"I will try to make this trip a short one," he said. "I'll be back before you know it."

"Thank you for your concern," I said formally. "When will you be leaving?"

He shook his head. "Not for a few days; it all depends, really." He didn't say on what, and there seemed little point in asking him. There was one thing I could clear up, however.

"Garth, did you tell Lucy to burn the papers that were here?"

He looked me full in the face so that I felt a little uncomfortable under his uncompromising stare.

"Yes, Catherine, I did. They were none of your business. Did you read any of them?"

I shook my head. "No; I must confess that I had little opportunity. I would have read them, had they still been here today."

He nodded. "Very well then; forget all about them.

Pretend they never existed." He smiled. "The portrait you may keep."

"Thank you," I said, genuinely pleased. "I'm sure, from the quality of the brushwork and the delicate use of color, that the painting must be of some value."

He shrugged. "It is of no use to me. If it gives you pleasure, you are welcome to it."

He opened the door then. "I'll leave you to rest, Catherine. Perhaps if you stay in your room for a time, I can have a private word with my brother."

The door closed behind him, and all the warmth I had felt when Garth gave me the portrait was dispelled by his curt request that I keep out of the way. I sank down in my chair and closed my eyes. Would I ever understand the undercurrents that seeped like dangerous mists into the very walls of Langland Hall?

The day of the party dawned clear and bright. I was awake early, heartened to see that the beating rain and high winds had given way to soft, spring-like sunshine.

I hurried down to the kitchens as soon as I was dressed. Cook was already busy over the ovens, and the delicious smell of baking bread made my mouth water.

"Are you managing all right?" I asked, stepping quickly out of her way as she brought a steaming tray over to the table.

"I manage better on my own," she said with a twinkle in her eyes.

148

Taking the hint, I retreated back upstairs and decided to take a short walk around the gardens. It was good to see the cloudless sky above the changing blue of the sea, and I breathed deeply of the warm air.

Jonathon joined me in the garden. He seemed in excellent spirits, his bright hair hanging over his forehead so that he looked little more than a boy.

"You must have picked the weather out yourself!" I smiled up at him, and he took my arm. "I hope it will be a very good party."

"It will be the best," he said with conviction. "You will like the Doctor and his wife, I'm sure, and Mr. Sainsbury, of course you know." He tipped back his head and stared up at the sky.

"The schoolteacher is a bit of a dry stick, but his wife makes up for him; she is very witty. Yes, I think it will be a memorable evening."

Suddenly Garth's voice broke the silence of the morning.

"Jonathon," he called, "would you come inside for a moment? There is something I wish to discuss with you."

I felt Jonathon stiffen. "You would think he was calling to his hounds," he said in a fury. "I will not be spoken to in that way."

He hurried across the grass, and after a moment I heard the two brothers arguing heatedly with each other. I sighed. Would they never learn to act like grown men?

I made up my mind that I would keep well out of the way of both of them during the day. Perhaps the party would put them in a better mood.

The day passed slowly, but at last it was time for me to go upstairs and dress. Lucy came to pin up my hair, and when I stepped into the blue gown, the result surprised even me.

"Oh, Miss Catherine!" Lucy said, standing back to see me the better. "You look like a princess, you really do."

I laughed at Lucy's generous praise, but all the same I was delighted by the way the gown clung to me in all the right places, the changing blue of the silk complementing the color of my hair.

"Every man in the room will fall in love with you," Lucy breathed romantically, and I giggled.

"I hope not, or I'll have some irate wives to deal with! All I want is a peaceful life."

To my surprise, Jonathon was waiting at the foot of the stairs for me, his eyes alight as he watched my descent.

"Perfect," he said. "You look every inch the lady of the manor. Won't you think again about becoming my wife?"

I put my hand on his arm. "Jonathon, we have no time to discuss our private affairs." I smiled in what I hoped was a kindly way. "We must be ready to greet our guests."

The dining room was beautiful. Lights from the

candles flickered onto the silverware and turned the crystal glass into sparkling diamonds. Whatever else the townspeople might think of us, they would know we kept a good table at the Hall.

The guests arrived together, no doubt having joined company on the dark road to the Hall. The ladies were a little distant, but the menfolk talked loudly and jovially, so that there were no uncomfortable silences.

The doctor's wife appraised my gown with sharp eyes as we took our places at the table. No doubt she was searching for evidence of the wantonness that she had probably been led to expect from me.

I looked across at Garth, who was deep in conversation with Mr. Sainsbury, his dark head bent forward. He looked extremely handsome, and my heart skipped a beat as he looked up and our eyes met.

"Mr. Llewellyn is a fine-looking man." The doctor's wife spoke quietly at my side, voicing my own thoughts, and the telltale color rose to my cheeks.

"Yes, he is. Both my cousins are handsome, don't you think?" I said cautiously.

Her eyes were speculative, as if she were considering the possibility of Jonathon being my lover as well as Garth.

Without any warning, the door burst open and Daniel Perkins stood on the threshold of the room, gripping the arm of his white-faced daughter.

In the sudden silence, my eyes were drawn to Sarah's gown. It was an exact replica of mine, made of the same shimmering silk, and suddenly I felt ill.

Garth rose to his feet. "Have you any business you wish to discuss with me, Perkins?" His voice was like ice. "If so, we shall retire to the study and leave our guests in peace."

Perkins smiled unpleasantly. "It would suit you very well to hustle me out of the way, wouldn't it?"

"I don't know what you mean," Garth said with composure, looking to where Jonathon, white of face, was leaning on the table as if for support.

Perkins drew Sarah into the center of the room. She looked around at the assembled guests, a defiant tilt to her head.

"Tell these fine people what you have told me this night, miss; go on before I whip you!"

He pulled at his daughter's arm, and I felt sorry for her. She looked mutely at him, shaking her head. He raised his hand, but Garth spoke sharply.

"I'll have none of that here, Perkins! Lay a hand on the girl, and you'll have me to answer to."

"All right!" Perkins shouted. "If the slut won't talk, then I will." He spun around to face me, and I remained frozen in my chair, quite unable to move.

"You are the one that's caused all the trouble!" he said venomously, and I stared at him in astonishment. "You are supposed to be Llewellyn's woman, yet you let him make a fool of a simple girl like my Sarah." He stared at Garth once more.

"Don't pretend you are innocent. My daughter is

152

going to have your child!'' He threw Sarah a contemptuous look.

"She didn't know it, but I had my suspicions weeks ago. Well, Mr. Llewellyn, what do you say to that?''

Garth turned to the guests. "In the circumstances, perhaps it would be better for us to meet some other time. My apologies to you all.''

There was no alternative but for the guests to take a decent departure, though I could see that the doctor's wife was agog with curiosity. No doubt the tale would be all over the town by morning.

Suddenly the room was cleared, and Sarah burst into hysterical tears.

"Why have you brought disgrace to me?'' she said to Garth, holding out her hands in supplication.

"Very pretty,'' he said with sarcasm, "But save it; the audience is gone now.'' He indicated that Daniel should take a seat.

"There is nothing to be gained by trying to blackmail me,'' he said calmly. "I have no intention of supporting your daughter or her bastard child.''

Perkins flushed a dull red, and Sarah looked at him with abject fear. "The child is his, Father!'' she said quickly. "I have not lied to you.''

Garth ignored her and turned to me. "I think you should go to your room, Catherine,'' he said quietly. "There is no reason for you to witness this unpleasantness.''

I was too shocked and too weary to answer. I rose to

my feet and stumbled up the stairs to my room.

When I was alone, the tears spilled down my cheeks, and I fell face downward on the bed, caring nothing for the fact that my gown was being crushed. There was no joy in it now.

A few minutes later, I heard Perkins' gruff voice in the hallway.

"All right then, Mr. Llewellyn. Just so my girl gets paid for her troubles, I'll be satisfied."

I closed my eyes in pain. So Garth had managed to buy his way out of the predicament without a thought about the child that was his.

As soon as the door closed on Perkins and his daughter, I hurried down the stairs. Garth was sitting slumped in a chair, and there was no sign of Jonathon.

"Garth," I said softly, "how could you allow yourself to be mixed up with such people?" He looked up slowly.

"So you believe Sarah Perkins, with no evidence against me at all except her word?"

I sat down quickly, feeling somewhat discomfited. "But it's not just her word," I said. "I heard Perkins talking to Mr. Sainsbury about it some weeks ago."

He raised his eyebrows. "I see," he said in a strange voice. He rose to his feet, and his glance flickered over me so coldly that I felt I was the one in the wrong. He walked past me without speaking another word, and I lay back in my chair, wondering why I should feel such a pang of guilt inside me.

FOURTEEN

I hardly saw Garth at all during the next few days, and I knew he was deliberately avoiding me. I couldn't shake off the feeling that somehow I'd failed him, even though I told myself repeatedly that the notion was a foolish one.

Jonathon had an air of triumph, a lightness in his step that I couldn't understand. It was almost as if he reveled in Garth's predicament.

He spent a great deal of time following me around the gardens, popping up when I least expected him, paying me absurd compliments so that I dreaded to see him.

He trapped me one day in the rose arbor, putting his hands around my waist playfully.

"Come along, Catherine. Surely you are not made of stone. I'll make you marry me yet!"

His words brought a chill with them, so that I shuddered as I tried to draw away from him.

"I don't think I'm the marrying kind." I attempted to laugh, but he wasn't to be put off.

"There is no one else, is there? Surely you can think nothing of Garth after all that's happened?"

I evaded his question. "I'm quite happy to live here with both you and Garth to look after me."

He turned a little sulky. "Garth will not be here much longer."He turned away from me, and I caught his arm.

"What do you mean, Jonathon. Is he going away?"

He frowned. "The people of the town are incensed at his behavior with Sarah Perkins. Not only that, but he repeatedly acts at variance with the law. He can't be allowed to get away with it forever."

"There is no proof against him. There can't be, or he would not be free at this moment," I said in agitation.

Jonathon gave me a strange look. "There will be proof enough; just you wait and see."

Suddenly frightened, I moved away from him. "I think I'll take a walk," I said quickly." The fresh air might clear my mind."

"Keep to the road then, Catherine," he warned. "I have told you many times that the cliffs can be dangerous."

It seemed as if he were warning me of a greater danger than I could foresee, and I knew I was shivering.

The air was spicy with the scent of early flowers, and as I walked I regained a little of my serenity. I had not previously been given to bouts of hysteria or foolish fancies, so why should I allow myself to be frightened now?

Of course there had been attacks on my life, there was no denying that. Even if the incident of the girth had been an accident, the attacker in my room had been real enough.

I sat on a boulder and tried to think of some motive for anyone wishing me dead. Chilled, I realized that Garth would be the beneficiary if anything happened to me. As the legitimate heir, he would no doubt have my money as well as his own share of Grandmother's estate. It was a point I should clear up with Mr. Sainsbury, of course, but I had the awful feeling I was right.

I rose and walked around the headland. Garth might be guilty of a lot of things, but surely he couldn't be capable of trying to murder me. Perkins worked for Garth, and it was only since the trouble with Sarah that I had seen any animosity between them.

A tall ship caught my eye, sweeping out to sea, its sails spread wide to catch every breath of wind. My heart dipped as I recognized the colors of the Sea Witch. I followed it along, wondering what Garth could be doing. I imagined him with his brown arms bare, leaning on the rail, so vital, so handsome. He could not be guilty of murder; I would not believe it of

157

him.

I longed to be in his arms, to hear his protestations of love as he held me close to him. But it was all a foolish dream.

The Sea Witch turned in a wide arc and headed back towards the Harbor, and I began to retrace my steps back to the Hall. I had reached no conclusion in my mind, but was resolved to find out as quickly as possible if it was Garth who would inherit my share of the estate.

Dinner that evening was an uncomfortable affair. The two men stared at each other in silence, and all my attempts at conversation met with the barest of replies. I gave up at last and ate my meal in silence.

As soon as possible, I made my way upstairs on the feeble pretense that I was developing a headache. My cousins rose politely to their feet as I left the table, but neither of them made any attempt to detain me.

I had only just settled myself close to the window in an attempt to do some needlework when I heard the sound of raised voices from below.

My heart beat uncomfortably fast as Garth's deep voice rose in anger. I dropped my needlework to the floor and crept out to the head of the stairs, straining to hear what was being said. I was terrified that the brothers might come to blows.

"How can you be so hard and unfeeling toward the girl?" Jonathon's voice rang out, and breathlessly I waited for Garth to reply.

"If Sarah Perkins is in trouble, then she had better not come wailing to me to help her!" Garth sounded furious. "She went into this affair with her eyes open. I have promised her father money; what more can be expected of me? It is none of my concern what happens now."

I was appalled at his cruelty. Could he not imagine how humiliated the girl must be and how afraid she was of her brute of a father?

Sick at heart, I crept back to my room and closed the door. Nothing could be gained by any interference from me. I would be unable to hide my contempt from Garth, and that would only serve to anger him more.

It was a long time before the shouting ceased, and even when the building was quiet, I lay wide-eyed in my bed. I doubted now that I had ever known anything at all about the character of my cousin Garth.

Lucy was agog with gossip when, heavy-eyed, I made my way down to breakfast. She carried in the tea tray, her hands shaking with excitement.

"Have you heard about Sarah Perkins, miss?" she said, knowing full well I hadn't. "She's run off in the middle of the night. Poor thing, and her going to have a child, too."

I looked at her, startled. "Doesn't anyone know where she has gone?" I asked. Lucy shook her head.

"Oh, no, she wouldn't leave any clues behind, because if her father catches up with her, he'll whip her within an inch of her life, baby or no baby."

"But I thought him the sort of man who would be delighted to have her off his hands," I said in surprise.

Lucy rubbed her hands on her apron. "Not until he has his money from Mr. Garth, he wouldn't."

I saw the truth of this. "I can't help feeling sorry for the poor girl—" I sighed—"although I could never bring myself to like her."

Lucy sniffed. "Not many could, miss, so you are not alone in that. She flaunted herself before the men; it's not a bit of wonder she ended up like she did."

Lucy moved to the door. "One thing puzzles me, though. Where would the likes of her get money to run away?" She sniffed again. "No doubt she smiled at some man or other."

I remembered the fifty pounds that had been taken from my bag when I was at the Perkins' house. Sarah had plenty of money; there was no need to worry on that score.

I gave up any pretense of eating and rose from the table. This would be a good time to try to see Mr. Sainsbury; neither of my cousins was around to stop me.

I was putting on my cloak when Lucy came up behind me with an exclamation of surprise.

"Where are you going, Miss Catherine? I've had

orders to see that you remain indoors."

"I'm sorry if I get you into any trouble, Lucy," I said with a smile. "I have to go into town on a little errand. I promise I'll be as quick as I can."

She darted away, and after a few moments Cook came up the stairs, breathing heavily from the exertion.

She had quickly pulled on a faded brown cloak over her spotless apron, and she smiled a little sourly at me.

"If you are going to town, Miss Catherine, I'm coming too," she said with such determination that I knew she wouldn't be moved.

I shrugged. "Very well; come if you must."

I helped her into the trap, and she plumped herself down, nearly tipping the small carriage with her weight. "I'll walk," I said, and off we went, the strangest-looking procession imaginable.

It was a nice day, and sooner than I thought we came to the dipping road leading into the town. Cook was still sitting like a brooding spider, and hiding a smile, I stopped the pony outside Mr. Sainsbury's office.

I had not seen him since the night of the dinner party, and he avoided my eyes as he held a chair for me to sit down.

"What can I do for you, young lady?" he asked with a great show of joviality.

"I just want to know the answer to a simple

161

question, Mr. Sainsbury," I said, coming straight to the point. "Who will benefit from Grandmother's will after my death?"

He seemed a little nonplused. "Why, the legitimate heir, of course, though if you marry, you must make a will leaving the money to your children. Otherwise it will naturally belong to your husband."

"But," I said, determined to be clear, "if I were to die now, Garth Llewellyn would benefit?"

He nodded. "Precisely, dear lady." He beamed at me over the top of his spectacles. "Is there anything you wish me to draft for you, a will or something?"

I shuddered and shook my head. "No, not yet." I gave him a wry look and rose to my feet. "That is all I wanted to know."

Cook was still waiting patiently for me, and as I left Mr. Sainsbury's office she waved her fist at some children who had come around to look at me.

I took the reins and led the pony and trap away from the town and up the cliff road back to the Hall. I shivered and passed quickly by the place where I had been set upon by thugs, though anyone who chanced attacking me with Cook there would be asking for trouble.

I smiled at her warmly, and she looked away, but not before I'd seen the humor in her eyes. It was a longer journey going back. The gallant pony strained upwards, and I did my best to help him by pushing the side of the trap. At last, when we were both almost exhausted, the road flattened out, and the Hall came in sight.

"I think that calls for a small glass of brandy," I said breathlessly to Cook when we were inside. She made no attempt to protest, but took the glass from my hand and drained it with very little effort.

When she returned to the kitchen, I sank down in a chair, my legs weak with tiredness, my head full of spinning thoughts. Garth wanted me dead. There was no other explanation for everything that had happened. He was the one who would benefit financially.

I wanted to cry, but even as the tears burned behind my eyes, Lucy came into the room, a strange look on her face.

"You have a visitor, miss," she said excitedly. "You'll never guess who it is; not in a hundred years you won't."

I coughed a little and sat up straight, trying to concentrate on what she was saying.

"Who is it, Lucy? Since I cannot guess, you'd better tell me, hadn't you?"

She came toward me, her eyes wide. "It's Sarah Perkins, miss," she said in a whisper. "She says she wants you to help her!"

It was a strange situation. I had just discovered that Garth would probably stop at nothing to be rid of me, and here was Sarah, who was carrying his child,

163

wanting my help.

"You'd better show her in, Lucy," I said quickly. "It might be dangerous if anyone sees her here."

"She's a bad lot, that one," Lucy warned. "Send her away, miss. I feel something awful will happen if you give her shelter here."

For a moment I was tempted to listen to Lucy. It was as much as I could do to cope with my own troubles without taking on those of anyone else.

I hesitated, but just for a fraction of a second; then I looked up at Lucy.

"Show her in," I said flatly.

FIFTEEN

Sarah was a sight to arouse pity in the hardest of hearts. There were dark rings beneath her eyes, and her pretty blonde hair was bedraggled.

She stood at the door, her shoulders drooping, her whole demeanor one of abject hopelessness.

"Come inside," I said at once, torn with pity. "Warm yourself before the fire. Lucy will bring you a hot drink."

Sarah sank down into a chair, her eyes wary, like a dog who has been kicked so often that it trusts no one. She glanced up at me, and for a moment there was a touch of defiance in her eyes.

"I had to come here," she said. "There was no one who would help me." She clenched her hands together. "I haven't a penny to bless myself with; I don't know what I am going to do."

I sat opposite her. "I will help you, Sarah." I bit my lip. "Surely you still have some of the fifty pounds. You did take it from my bag, didn't you?"

She flushed a deep scarlet. "I didn't mean to keep

165

it; I just wanted to upset you." She couldn't look at me. "Father found out I had it and he kept it; he said Jonathon owed him money in any event." She managed to look up at me, her lips trembling. "I have to get away, or my father will kill me!"

"Don't let yourself become hysterical," I said crisply. "I know your father is a hard man, but there is no need to exaggerate the situation." I paused for a moment. "Anyway, I thought that Garth was going to pay your father some sort of compensation."

She flashed me a look that I couldn't understand. "You haven't much sense, for all that you are a fine lady," she said flatly. "Mr. Garth will give my father a small sum, but he will not be pushed too far."

I gave an exclamation of impatience. "Well, Garth should have considered all the difficulties before he took advantage of you."

She shook her head in disbelief. "Surely you've guessed it by now?" She stared at me, and I felt uncomfortable. She gave a short laugh. "The child isn't Mr. Garth's. I only wish it was; at least he's a man."

I stood up quickly, my heart beating so quickly I felt almost suffocated. I stared unseeingly through the window, wondering if she could be telling the truth this time.

"But he gave you the silk, the same silk he gave me. Why should he do that?"

She withered me with a glance. "Fancy you not realizing the truth. There was a lot of silk left over from the bolt, and my mother is clever with a needle, as you know. She just sewed the pieces together and made a dress for me."

"I suppose I have been rather stupid." I stared at her. "Why didn't Garth deny the fact that he was the father of your child? Why did he allow everyone to believe he was responsible?"

She clucked her tongue. "To protect his precious brother, of course. He's always been the same, because Jonathon is so much younger, I suppose. Mr. Garth is more of a man than ever Jonathon could be."

There was a knock at the door, and Lucy came in with a tray. "The toddy, miss."

Sarah pressed her lips firmly together. She obviously had no intention of saying any more while Lucy was in the room. When she left the room, Sarah sat up straighter in her chair, her cheeks pink.

"Nosy slut!" she said. "I expect she'll go and tell everyone that I was up here at the Hall. My father will soon be after me then."

"Calm yourself, Sarah, please," I said firmly. "Lucy isn't going to gossip about you, so don't fret."

I stared at her, trying to establish how much of her story I could believe. One thing was certain: if her father caught up with her, the least she could expect was a good hiding.

167

She was watching my face. "It's true about Mr. Jonathon," she said rather testily. "He was always spoiled. His grandmother wrote him letter upon letter, often sending him gifts of money. I expect everyone wanted to make up to him for being born a bastard, if you'll excuse me for saying it, miss."

I took a quick sip of my drink, trying to sort things out in my mind. Jonathon had denied even hearing from Grandmother, let alone receiving money from her.

"My father told me that Mr. Garth's mother was never liked because she was some sort of foreigner, so most of the family money was left to Jonathon."

"Did you imagine Jonathon would marry you?" I asked a little coldly, and she flushed.

"No, I never expected that. But I thought he would set me up in a little home of my own, look after me and the child." Tears came to her eyes. "I didn't know he was little more than a child himself, in his mind anyway."

I came to a decision suddenly, persuaded that now, perhaps for the first time, she was telling the truth.

"I'll help you, Sarah," I said. "But it will take time for me to raise some money." I managed a smile. "At least Jonathan owes you that much."

I moved to the door. "You go upstairs and wait in my room. It will take me an hour or two to get the money from Mr. Sainsbury."

168

She clutched her hands together. "Oh, what if my father comes looking for me? This is the first place he'll look."

"Lock yourself in," I said practically. "Or come into town with me."

She shook her head. "No, I couldn't face all those nosy faces looking at me." She choked a little on the words. "I'll be glad to get away from here, that I will." She looked at me.

"You should think about going away for a while, too, miss. My father can be a very dangerous man."

"I believe you," I said. "But nothing can be gained by my running away."

I led the way upstairs to my room. I saw Lucy stare in, but she said nothing until I returned to the hallway.

"You are not going to trust her alone in your room, miss?" she asked. "She would steal the clothes off your back, would that one."

"I know you don't like her, Lucy," I said, trying to be calm. "But she is in trouble, after all."

"She's a bad lot, Miss Catherine, and you are too trusting by far. I don't trust any of the Perkins family, and that's the truth."

"Why are you so bitter against them?" I asked in surprise, and Lucy rubbed her hands on her apron.

"All I know is that Mr. Jonathon hasn't been himself since he's been mixed up with that bunch.

He's an evil man, is that Perkins, and I've no doubt his daughter's the same."

I pulled my cloak around me, trying to disregard the chill that suddenly went through me. "I have to go into town, Lucy. I won't be very long."

Her eyes widened. "But, miss, you shouldn't go into town alone. You know Mr. Garth said you were to stay here."

I hesitated for a moment, biting my lip in an agony of indecision. I did not relish a repetition of the horrible business of the attack upon me by some of the thugs off the docks.

"Give me a note, Miss Catherine," she said with determination. "It would be better for me to go." She saw my hesitation. "Don't worry about me, miss. No one will bother me; why should they?"

Convinced, I hastily penned a note to Mr. Sainsbury, asking him for some money, and Lucy tucked it into her pocket.

"Here," I said, swinging my own cloak onto her shoulders, "and please be careful, Lucy."

I watched her dumpy figure disappear down the road with some trepidation, returning to the sitting room with a feeling of loneliness and of impending doom that was hard to shake off.

Upstairs, I could hear Sarah walk across the landing, and it cheered me a little to know that she was in the house; not that she could be described as a pleasant companion by any stretch of the imagination.

I sat down before the fire and leaned back in my chair, closing my eyes with a sigh of weariness. I think I must have dozed for a moment, because I opened my eyes to find Sarah standing before me, a hard look on her face.

"I thought you had gone into town to get me some money." Her voice was accusing, and I fought down the feeling of anger that rose within me.

"You fool!" she said, almost beside herself. "Go now before it grows too dark!"

"Don't you dare to use that tone to me," I said, striving to be calm. "You are up to something, my girl. What is it?"

She sank down onto a chair, pressing her hands to her lips. "I tried to help you, but you wouldn't listen. Well, no one can blame me for anything that happens to you now!"

I caught her wrist in my hand. "What are you talking about? Is your father perhaps on his way here to finish off what he started the night he attacked me with a knife?"

Her eyes almost started out of her head. She jerked her hand away, almost pulling me off my feet. She was a big girl, much stronger than I was. She gave me a push, and I stumbled, caught off my guard. She ran to the door and flung it open and was running along the cliff road before I could do anything to stop her.

When I could see there was no hope of her returning, I bolted the door carefully. I hurried downstairs to warn Cook that the back door should be locked, too. The room was empty. A fire glowed in the big hearth, and the hobs were covered with cooking pots, but there was no sign of Cook.

Shaking a little, I slid the heavy bolts of the back door into position and checked to see if the windows were securely closed. I was not going to take the chance of someone creeping in without me knowing about it.

I lit plenty of candles, my heart beating rather quickly as I looked round the empty, shadow-filled rooms. I tried to bolster my courage by telling myself that Lucy would be returning soon.

I sat near the window, watching as the shadows lengthened along the garden, making weird, frightening shapes on the grass. Soon it became too dark for me to see anything, and with a swift gesture of panic, I jerked the drapes shut.

The big clock in the hall chimed; the sound seemed to echo in the silence of the hallway. I prayed that Garth would return, that soon I would hear the ring of a horse's hooves in the cobbled yard; anything to break the silence that was all around me.

I could not bear it any longer. I searched in a cupboard and found a lantern, and with its light as company, opened the door and set off across the grass.

I stumbled as I came to the cobbled yard leading to the stables. A frightening silence greeted me. There were none of the usual sounds of restless hooves against the straw or the soft, sleepy noises of animals bedded down for the night.

I held the lantern high and, as I had expected, the stalls were empty. It seemed clear someone had intended that I should be alone at the Hall with no means of escape.

I squared my shoulders. I would not be beaten; I would not remain there waiting to be murdered! I stepped out quickly, before my courage could desert me, in the direction of the cliff road.

SIXTEEN

There was a depth to the darkness that left me breathless with fear. The lantern gave very little light and yet had the disadvantage of leaving me an easy target for anyone who wished to harm me.

I tried to quicken my pace over the uneven ground and sank into marshy wetness, screaming a little with cold and shock as I scrambled onto firm soil again.

I seemed to be completely lost. I had started out with the intention of making my way to the dockside in an effort to find Garth. But now there was just one thought in my mind: to put as much ground as possible between Langland Hall and myself.

The wind was rising, and I shivered, wishing I'd had the sense to stop long enough to pull on a cloak. The material of my dress was thin and tore easily as I blundered into bushes. I did not even feel the pain as the brambles scratched my skin, so anxious was I to reach a place of safety.

Suddenly I missed my footing and was sprawled out on the hard earth, the breath knocked from my body.

Wincing with pain, I tried to rise, but it was no use. I had twisted my foot so severely that I could hardly move.

I sank down with a soft moan. The lantern had been broken in the fall, and now I was in complete darkness. I huddled into a hollow and wrapped my arms around myself in an effort to keep warm, but tears were very near the surface.

After a while, the cold and darkness began to play on my nerves. I imagined there were footsteps around me, faces peering at me with eyes shining yellow like a cat's. I forced myself to my feet and hobbled a few steps, trying desperately to find the roadway.

I stopped for breath, leaning against a tree, the throbbing of my ankle forcing me to throw caution to the wind. I flung back my head and called at the top of my voice: "Help!"

The sound seemed to echo through the darkness, and I called again. "Is anyone there?"

After a few minutes I thought I heard a faint answering voice. In a frenzy of excitement I shouted again and again until my voice was almost gone.

There was perspiration on my face, in spite of the fact that I was shivering. I waited tensely, clinging to the rough bark of the tree, and then I heard a voice, nearer this time.

"Miss Catherine, is that you?" Almost faint with relief, I recognized Lucy's familiar tones. Then, like a miracle, she was looming up out of the darkness, a lantern swinging from her hand.

"Oh, miss, whatever are you doing here?" She caught my arm, and I knew there were tears of relief on my cheeks.

"Never mind that now, Lucy. Did you see Mr. Sainsbury? Did you see Mr. Garth?"

She shook her head. "I didn't see anyone, miss; the town seems to be deserted. There was nothing to do but to return home."

My hopes fell. "No one knows we are up here alone, then?" I said a little desperately. "Sarah has run off. It's possible that her father intends to come up to the Hall, and he's not the person I most want to see at this moment!"

"Well, miss, I think we should make our way back to the Hall. You're shivering in that dress, and what have you done to your foot?"

I shrugged. "I've sprained my ankle, I think. You're right, of course; we'd better go back. Do you think you can find the way?"

Lucy smiled. "Lord bless you, miss, I've known these hills and fields ever since I was a little girl. I know them like the back of my hand."

It was a long, painful journey, but with Lucy supporting me on one side, we at last came to the arched doorways of the Hall.

"Look, Lucy!" I said excitedly. "There are fresh candles in the windows; Garth must be home."

I pushed open the door and saw with a swift sense of

disappointment that it was Jonathon standing there.

He took my arm, helping me into the sitting room. He was pale and seemed to be very nervous. He kept darting looks over his shoulder as if expecting someone to loom up behind him.

"Where's Garth?" I asked hopefully. "Is he on his way home?" Jonathon licked his lips, shaking his head.

"I don't know where he is," he said, going over to the brandy and pouring some for himself. He glanced at Lucy, and I nodded my head to her.

"Make us a pot of tea, Lucy, and bring a cup in for yourself."

When she left the room, I stared at Jonathon, waiting for him to say something. He gulped the brandy nervously, his eyes looking anywhere but at me.

"Sarah has been here," I said, breaking the strained silence. "She told me a great deal."

He closed his lips like a mutinous child and did not answer.

"She said you were the father of her child," I persisted, "and that you would not help her in any way."

"Why should I help her!" He almost spat the words out. "She thought she would bring the baby up as a Llewellyn, to share in our fortune, the scheming little hussy."

I stared at him for a moment. He seemed more

excitable than ever; his hands shook so that he could hardly hold his glass.

"Sarah told me that Perkins was on his way up to the Hall. What does he want, Jonathon—to kill me to get me out of the way?"

He crumpled visibly at the mention of Perkins' name, looking around as if expecting him to appear at any moment. I took his arm, drawing him toward me.

"What hold has that man got over you? Can't you tell me, Jonathon?" In spite of myself, my voice shook.

He bent toward me suddenly, his eyes shining brightly, his hand feverishly hot as it rested on mine.

"Get away from here now, Catherine, while you can!" he said in an urgent whisper. "Grandmother should never have sent you here, never should have entrusted the money to you."

I stared up at him. "You will have your share, Jonathon," I said, suddenly frightened by the odd way he was behaving. "If I should die, the money would go to Garth. I asked Mr. Sainsbury about it."

Lucy came in with the tray of tea, but Jonathon appeared not to see her.

"No, that is where you are wrong, Catherine. Mr. Sainsbury did not tell you the truth." He brushed his hand over his face. "I am the one who will inherit the money, Catherine. And if Perkins can manage it, I'll have Garth's share, too."

Lucy put down the tray. "It's true, miss," she said quietly. "I burned the paper myself in your own fireplace. Mr. Jonathon does get the money to handle if you should die."

"Lucy," I said with sudden determination, "you must get out of this house. Warn Garth that he is in danger, and send someone up for me, if you can."

She edged toward the door. But with a sudden lunge, Jonathon hit her in the face, and she dropped to the ground like a stone.

"I can't allow you to do that, Catherine." Jonathon's eyes were no longer rational. I dropped to my knees, terrified that Lucy might be dead, but she was still breathing.

Jonathon leaned forward and dragged Lucy into the hallway. I heard a cupboard door open and then a thump as he pushed her inside. In any event, she would be safe there if she would only remain silent.

Jonathon came back and stood looking down at me regretfully. He was pale, with a fine beading of sweat on his forehead.

"I'm sorry, Catherine!" he said, and I watched in horror as he sank down onto his knees.

"Perkins will bleed me white!" he said bitterly. "He intends to be rich, and the devil take me or anyone else who tries to stand in his way."

There was a sound outside the window of heavy feet crunching against the cobbles. I froze into silence, and Jonathon stared as if in a trance at the door.

In horror, as if in a nightmare, I watched the handle turn. And then, as the door was flung wide, Perkins stepped into the room.

I looked at Jonathon imploringly. Surely he would not allow Perkins to harm me. He struggled to his feet and rushed across the room.

"Give me the stuff, Perkins, I beg of you. I'll go mad if I don't have some soon."

"You will wait until I am ready," Perkins said arrogantly, and I longed to strike him. He looked at me and grinned evilly.

"Do you know how it is I have the power to make your fool of a cousin dance like a puppet on a string?" he asked, full of his own importance.

"I think I can hazard a guess," I said with a feeling of horror. Jonathon attempted to pour himself another drink, but his hand was shaking so badly that the decanter slipped from his hand and the wine spilled like blood over the carpet.

I started to rise, but Perkins waved me back into my seat.

"Oh, no you don't, young lady; you just stay where you are so that I can keep my eye on you."

He clicked his fingers at Jonathon. "Get more wine, and I will have some, too."

While he was looking at my cousin, I picked up the heavy silver teapot and struck out with it. Unfortunately, Perkins must have spotted the gleam out of the corner of his eye and moved, receiving only a glancing blow.

With an oath, he snatched the teapot and flung it

against the wall, where it shattered a mirror and fell to the ground with a terrible noise.

"Take care!" he said menacingly. "These are the last few moments of your life; why not enjoy them?"

"If you are going to kill me, why not have it over and done with!" I said, my voice rising hysterically. He leaned back in his chair and smiled at me.

"When I'm ready," he said cruelly. "But first I want you to know how clever I am."

Jonathon returned with a fresh bottle of wine and managed to pour two glasses without spilling it. Perkins looked at him with scorn. "Well, bring it here, and don't be all night about it!"

"Please," Jonathon begged, "give me the opium now."

I looked at him with a mixture of horror and compassion. It was true, then, that my cousin was bringing about his own downfall.

"It's like this, Miss Llewellyn," Perkins said smoothly. "Your cousin has been doing business with me for some time now." He paused, his eyes on Jonathon. "It was a good arrangement. I would arrange for illicit cargo to be brought in on Garth Llewellyn's ships and dispose of it to the highest bidder."

He took a drink of his wine, and I sat in silence, more frightened than I had ever been in my life.

"Things were going very smoothly," Perkins continued, "until your lily-livered cousin started doping himself up on opium." He grinned again. "It suited me down to the ground; we were bringing in more and more contraband cargo." He chuckled. "We almost had more of that than genuine ship-ments."

I found my voice. "It was all right until Garth found you out, I suppose?"

"Well," Perkins said, "he was suspicious, but he had to be careful because his precious brother was involved. Which was all to the good, I thought."

"You are not going to get away with this!" I said in sudden anger. "Jonathon would be a fool to give you the money, even if you succeed in murdering me. He would be signing his own death warrant!"

Perkins took out a package from under his coat and held it up before Jonathon's face.

"He has already signed his death warrant himself," he said as Jonathon made a lunge for the package. Perkins pulled it away. "While I have this, your cousin will sign any papers I ask him to. Soon I will be rich, can't you see?"

"Jonathon!" I said urgently. "Once you sign anything, Perkins will get rid of you, too, can't you understand that? Please, Jonathon, try to see what is happening!"

"That's enough of that!" Perkins said roughly, raising his hand as if to strike me. "You sorely tempt me to kill you now."

"Go ahead!" I shouted, forgetting my fear for a

moment. "Do your worst, and see what good it will do you! Garth will never give in to your demands!"

"You may be right," he said. "One thing I'll say for you: you have more spirit in you than that whelp of mine. Screeched like a stuck pig, she did."

I stared at him, unable to believe the horror of his words.

"Do you mean to tell me that you have killed Sarah?" I asked in terror, my blood running cold at his callousness.

"Of course I killed the slut!" he said. "I had no intention of letting her bear another Llewellyn so that she could claim some of the estate."

Perkins smiled at his own cleverness, and I turned away from him in disgust. It would be of no use to try to appeal to his better nature; he did not have one.

Suddenly Jonathon, who had been standing almost in a daze, listening to us, moved forward, a pistol in his hand.

"Give me the packet," he said loudly. "Give it to me before I kill you."

Perkins spun around, a look of frightened cunning on his face.

"Come, give the pistol to me," he said coaxingly. "How will you manage to get your opium if I am not around to help you?"

Jonathon's hand wavered for a moment. "Don't listen to him!" I said urgently. "I will help you, Jonathon."

He looked at me for a brief moment, and then Perkins was upon him, grappling for the firearm. I stood rooted to the spot, unable to move.

There was a sharp retort, and the two men seemed frozen together for a moment. Then Jonathon slid slowly to the ground, his eyes on me and his lips framing the word, "Sorry."

I tried to run then, though every step was like a red-hot poker driving into my foot. I knew that Perkins would soon be after me, and I was almost crying with terror when I saw a horse gently nibbling the grass of the lawn. It was probably Perkins' animal. Quickly I flung myself into the saddle and set off quickly in the direction of the road. I had to reach Garth; he would know what to do about Perkins.

I tried not to think of Jonathon, of the red stain slowly spreading over his coat. I shuddered and urged the animal on at a faster pace, thinking of the refuge I would find in Garth's arms.

Suddenly the animal stumbled as the sound of a shot echoed against the silent night. The stars in the sky seemed to spin in a frenzy of brilliance around my head. I hit the ground, and a deep blackness engulfed me.

SEVENTEEN

My head ached and my limbs were cramped, and as I slowly regained consciousness, I realized I was unable to move. There was a strange buzzing in my ears, and although I could feel the night wind on my arms, my face was covered with some coarse cloth so that I could scarcely breathe.

After a few moments, it became apparent that I was flung over the saddle of a horse. I felt sick with fear as I realized I was Daniel Perkins' prisoner. Perspiration beaded my face, and I strained to see through the blackness. Where was I being taken?

The animal jerked to a halt so suddenly that I felt myself begin to slide. I hit the ground with a bump. Even in my panic, I could smell tar and all the unmistakable scents of the docks.

I was hauled up roughly, and when I tried to struggle, a stunning blow was delivered to my face.

"Keep still, you vixen!" Perkins' tone was low and threatening. "Otherwise you will find yourself dropped straight into the ocean."

Obediently I stopped struggling, knowing there would be no hope for me, bound as I was, in the swiftly moving tide.

I could tell from Perkins' unsteady steps that we were boarding a ship, and I wondered for a moment why he was bothering to keep me alive at all.

After a moment, I was dropped unceremoniously onto the deck and fell forward, striking my face against the boards. Rough hands untied the cloth from my face, and thankfully I took a deep breath of the clean sea air.

Perkins, his arms crossed over his plump belly, stared down at me with triumphant eyes. He put out his foot and gave me a sharp kick which caught my shoulder painfully.

Anger flared through me, driving out terror. "Why not kill me now and get it over with?" I shouted. He clasped my face with his hand, his eyes glittering with menace.

"Utter another sound and you'll regret it," he said, and I knew he was capable of carrying out any threat he made.

"I have a use for you," he said. "You are a sprat to catch a mackerel, shall we say?" He grinned. "With Jonathon out of the way, I have to rely on Garth Llewellyn to give me his signature on certain documents."

"So you think you'll use me to trap him?" I said,

cold with fear. "He will not be so easily fooled."

Perkins laughed out loud. "You have a very poor opinion of your own charms, my dear. Oh, yes, I think I can get all I want from him in exchange for your life."

"But how will you find him?" I asked. "He is not at the Hall."

"He is now," Perkins said smugly. "He rode past me, just a few feet away from where we were hiding." He gave a cruel laugh. "But all he will find is his dead brother."

I shook my head. "But how can you hope to get away with it? Large sums of money are not so easy to raise all at once."

"That's where you are wrong, my dear young lady." Perkins folded his hands together, as pompous as a clergyman. "This is no spur-of-the-moment scheme; I have been planning it for some time." He peered at me with narrowed eyes. "Mr. Sainsbury agreed to give his cooperation for a price. Once I have the money, I shall be well away from here. You won't see my coattails for dust!"

"You won't get away with it," I said feebly, but I was trembling all over even as I spoke. There was a good chance of him getting away with it, and once the papers were signed, there would be no hope for Garth or me. Perkins would finish us off without hesitation.

He had lost interest in me now. "Take her down

into the hold," he said sharply to one of the seamen. "Keep her out of sight until I want her."

It was cold down below, and once the hatch was snapped into place, I began to look around for some means of freeing myself from the ropes that cut into my wrists.

I became aware of small scratching sounds and realized with a feeling of horror that there must be rats in the hold. I worked more desperately, fearful lest some of the creatures come near me.

After what seemed an endless time, I was free of the ropes. I rubbed my wrists, trying to bring some life back to my shaking fingers.

I looked round for a piece of pipe, anything that would make a suitable weapon. Holding my skirts high, I explored the hold, almost stumbling over a bundle of sailcloth. I pulled at it with all my strength and fell back a pace, too terrified even to scream. Feeling faint with nausea, I closed my eyes to the horror of what was lying there. Transfixed, I could not move, even when shrieking rats scampered in all directions away from the bundle. Sarah Perkins was dead. Her pale eyes, wide open, stared up at me as if in accusation, and there was dried blood on the bodice of her gown.

Shuddering, I threw the sailcloth back in place and, with an effort, moved away from the gruesome remains. I felt hysteria rise up in me, and I pressed my hand to my lips to stop from screaming out.

Perkins was a monster. No evil was too great for him; he had even stooped to killing his own daughter. I had not been willing to believe he was capable of cold-blooded murder, but the evidence was there before my eyes.

Suddenly the hold was opened, and before I had time to move, Perkins had me by the hair and was dragging me toward the deck.

Garth, white-faced, moved forward as if to take me in his arms, but Perkins waved a pistol at him.

"That's far enough," he said sourly. "When I have the money, the girl will be yours, not before."

"Don't believe him!" I cried. "Once you give your signature, he will kill us both."

Perkins raised his hand to strike me, and Garth moved quickly and silently, knocking the pistol to the ground and catching Perkins by his coat.

As Perkins fell, I thought for one glorious minute that I was free. I moved toward Garth, but hands grasped my throat, and I felt the sharpness of a blade against my back.

"Here are the documents; please sign them." Mr. Sainsbury sounded almost polite, and I had an insane desire to laugh. Perkins pushed himself up, a murderous gleam in his eyes. He caught my arm and twisted it so cruelly that I cried out, and I saw Garth pale visibly.

"Mr. Llewellyn, please sign. There will be no trouble; we do not want anyone to be hurt."

Mr. Sainsbury held out the documents imploringly, and Garth shook his head.

"You are a fool if you believe that," he said. "The moment you have what you want, Catherine and I will be dead."

We all stood quite still, each waiting for the other to make a move. And then on the night air came the strangest sound I'd ever heard.

I looked around fearfully, and it wasn't until a crowd of women carrying torches came into sight that I realized it was the sound of human voices.

They stood on the edge of the quay, their upturned faces ghostly under the light from their flares. At the front of the crowd stood Mrs. Perkins, and as she saw me she let out an animal howl.

"There she is!" she cried. "Burn the ship under her; burn the Sea Witch!"

The other women took up the cry until it filled the night with a chant that became almost inhuman as it rose to a crescendo. I shuddered. What had I ever done to arouse so much hate?

Even as the question was framed, I knew the answer. In Mrs. Perkins' mind, I had come between her daughter and her dreams of a profitable marriage, so she had poisoned other minds against me to help her in her revenge.

Someone threw a flare, and it landed on the dry timber of the ship, starting a blaze immediately. Another found its mark, and Garth moved with lightning speed, knocking Perkins to the deck and grasping my arm urgently.

Perkins started to rise and reached for his pistol, but Mr. Sainsbury was quicker than he.

"I cannot let you kill innocent people," he said, and calmly fired at point-blank range.

Garth drew me to the seaward side of the vessel. "Over the side, quickly!" he said. I hesitated just for a moment, frightened by the heavy swell of the sea.

"There is no other way out!" he urged, and with determination I hoisted up my petticoats and climbed over the rail.

Garth held onto my hand, lowering me gently. He was as agile as a monkey, but then, he had spent a lifetime aboard ships.

There was a ship waiting in the darkness below us, and thankfully I climbed into it, relieved not to have to face the sea after all.

Garth jumped in beside me, and then I saw the cook from Langland Hall grinning at us broadly.

"Once I knew what they were about, I thought I'd come and help you, Mr. Garth," she said cheerfully. "I always did have my work cut out keeping you out of mischief!"

Gasping, I lay in the bottom of the boat while Garth

steadily rowed out to sea, away from the burning ship. It burned fiercely, her pointing masts like red fingers lighing up the quayside.

Garth stopped rowing and put his arm around my shoulders.

"You look a sorry mess, don't you?"

He folded me in his arms, and despite the horror of the last few hours, I thrilled to him as I had always done.

"Your new ship," I said in a small voice. "You've lost her."

He tipped my face up to his. "I've learned that ships can be rebuilt. There are many ships, but only one woman."

We clung together then, with Cook smiling at us from her end of the boat.

"A fine pair of love birds," she said and, taking the oars, rowed steadily away from the roar of the burning ships.